"Maybe we shouldn't be walking off together."

"Why not?" Simon raised his eyebrows, wondering what she thought would happen if they took a walk together.

"Because your aunt and my grandmother are watching us."

He glanced toward them. Sure enough, they had their eyes on him and Lydia, and they were talking in low voices.

He shrugged. "So what?"

"Matchmaking," she said darkly.

He couldn't hold back a chuckle. "Come to think of it, I have seen a twinkle in Aunt Bess's eyes when she looks at us. But so what? They won't bother us, even if they chatter."

"You don't know them as well as you think if you believe that," she said, wrinkling her nose. "Once the two of them get started, they'll drive us crazy."

"All we have to do is ignore it, and they'll stop."

She paused and looked at him, her gaze pitying. "You poor thing. You really believe that."

They looked at each other, laughing a little, and he realized he felt a connection again, just as he had when she was a pesky little kid.

A lifetime spent in rural Pennsylvania and her Pennsylvania Dutch heritage led **Marta Perry** to write about the Plain People, who add so much richness to her home state. Marta has seen over seventy of her books published, with over seven million books in print. She and her husband live in a beautiful central Pennsylvania valley noted for its farms and orchards. When she's not writing, she's reading, traveling, baking or enjoying her six beautiful grandchildren.

Books by Marta Perry

Brides of Lost Creek

Second Chance Amish Bride
The Wedding Quilt Bride
The Promised Amish Bride
The Amish Widow's Heart
A Secret Amish Crush

An Amish Family Christmas
"Heart of Christmas"
Amish Christmas Blessings
"The Midwife's Christmas Surprise"

Visit the Author Profile page
at Harlequin.com for more titles.

A Secret Amish Crush

Marta Perry

LOVE INSPIRED

INSPIRATIONAL ROMANCE

LOVE INSPIRED®
INSPIRATIONAL ROMANCE

ISBN-13: 978-1-335-43083-0

A Secret Amish Crush

Copyright © 2021 by Martha P. Johnson

This edition published by arrangement with Harlequin Books S.A.

For questions and comments about the quality of this book, please contact us at CustomerService@Harlequin.com.

Love Inspired
22 Adelaide St. West, 40th Floor
Toronto, Ontario M5H 4E3, Canada
www.Harlequin.com

Printed in U.S.A.

Many waters cannot quench love,
neither can the floods drown it....
　　　　　　　　—*Song of Solomon* 8:7

This story is dedicated to the one who
walks with me through the storms of life:
my husband, Brian.

Chapter One

Lydia Stoltzfus had gotten only a mile down the road toward town when the first huge wet flakes began to fall. Several spattered Dolly's black coat, and the mare lifted her head, sniffed the air and gave a soft whicker.

"I know," Lydia said, as much to herself as to the mare. "We weren't supposed to get so much as a flake today. Maybe it will stop as soon as it started."

Driving another few hundred feet along the road was enough to convince her that hope was futile. The flakes had begun by melting on the narrow country road, but now they were sticking, and the sound of Dolly's hooves was muffled by their coating.

Should she keep going or turn back? Daad and Mammi would worry, that was certain sure, but how could she fail Elizabeth? Elizabeth Fisher, the elderly owner of the coffee shop where Lydia worked, had been sick off and on for most of the winter. She'd be relying on Lydia, and Lydia couldn't let her down.

Keeping a firm grip on the reins, Lydia tried to discourage Dolly's excited reaction to snow after what had been a fairly mild March. Those who had proclaimed an early spring in Lost Creek were going to be sadly disappointed, she feared.

"Komm, Dolly. Act your age." The mare was nearly as old as she was, and at twenty-five, Lydia was seeing even her best friends begin to use the word *maidal* in connection with her. Old maid.

A car went past, moving slowly in response to the increasingly slick road, and a sliver of apprehension slid through her. Still, Dolly was sure-footed, and she certain sure didn't get excited about traffic at her age. As long as they kept a steady pace, they should be fine.

Lydia had about three minutes to think that before she heard the sound of a car behind her—a car coming fast. She hugged the side of the road, hoping for the best. The driver was going much too fast for conditions, but there was plenty of room for the car to pass—

Without slowing, the vehicle rushed up on her. It was going to clear...but then, at the last possible moment, it clipped her wheel. She felt the buggy slide to the right and urged the mare back to the left, but it was too late. Lydia's right rear wheel slid off the road, and she felt the jolt of dropping down to the berm. Dolly, with a sudden return to good sense, came to a halt and there they sat, half on and half off the road.

Breathing a silent prayer of thanks

that they were both unhurt, Lydia assessed the situation. Would Dolly be able to get the buggy back onto the road or not? Shaking the lines, she tried to speak with more assurance than she felt. "Walk up, Dolly." She clucked at her. "You can do it."

Dolly made one half-hearted try and the buggy slid even farther. The mare halted, her ears back as if listening for a better idea.

"Stubborn creature." Lydia anchored the lines with a quick turn and slid cautiously down onto the wet surface. Slippery, very slippery underfoot. She moved slowly around the mare, patting her, to the offside.

"Komm along, girl." Grasping the headstall, she urged the mare to move forward. Dolly pawed with her forefeet, nervously testing the surface.

"Komm." Lydia tugged, the mare danced, the buggy rocked. And then Lydia's feet slid out from under her, she tried to right herself, and she landed flat on her face in the snow.

For an instant she lay there, stunned. Dolly reached down to nuzzle her, blowing warmly on her already wet face.

"Enough." Lydia pushed the mare's head out of the way and sat up. At least, she tried to sit up. It took two tries to make it happen, and then another three to get her up to standing.

Clinging to the harness, she caught her breath and tried to wipe the snow from her face. She hadn't quite finished when her ears caught the sound of another buggy coming up behind her. Relief swept through her. Help had come. Anyone with a buggy would be someone she knew.

The driver pulled up and slid down from the seat. Enos Fisher, who had the farm next to Daad's, came hurrying toward her, followed by another man.

"Ach, Lydia, what happened?" Enos

reached her, slithering a little on the wet surface.

"She's got herself into a pickle."

The swirling snow hid the other man's face, but she recognized the voice even though she hadn't heard it in years, and something in her jolted to attention. It was Simon, Enos's son. Several years her senior, he'd been the object of her schoolgirl crush back when she was a skinny kid and he was courting Rebecca Schultz. They'd married and disappeared out to an Ohio settlement, and she hadn't seen him since.

And now he was back, and his first impression of her would be that of a sopping wet female who couldn't even keep her buggy on the road.

Hoping her mortification didn't show in her face, Lydia glanced up, snow whirling between them. "We heard you were coming back, Simon. Wilkom." She hesitated, unsure of whether to mention the death of his wife or not.

Enos broke in before either of them could say another word. "Komm, Simon. We'll push, and Lydia, you get in and take the lines. We'll soon have you on the road again. You want to go home?"

She shook her head as she swung up to the seat. "I'm on my way to work. Elizabeth will be needing me."

"Gut. We're going there ourselves, so you can follow us. We'll see you there safe, won't we, Simon?"

Simon, looking to Lydia's eyes as if he'd rather do anything else, nodded and put his shoulder against the rear of the buggy. With both of them pushing and her urging Dolly on, she was back on the road in moments. Before she could even express her thanks, they'd gone back to their own buggy. Trying to ignore her wet clothes and the hair that was straggling from under her kapp, Lydia fell in behind them, and they were off.

The snow kept on coming down, but with another buggy to follow, she realized that both she and Dolly felt more comfortable. In another ten minutes they'd reached the coffee shop, driving down the alley alongside to the shed where the horses could be safe and comfortable.

Lydia had Dolly taken care of quickly, and as she moved past Enos's buggy, she spotted something she hadn't before. Or rather, someone. A little girl, bundled up in a winter jacket and mittens, snuggled under a carriage robe in the back seat. Simon's little girl, she'd guess.

She stopped next to the buggy, smiling. "Hello. I'm Lydia. What's your name?"

Wide blue eyes stared at her from a small, pale face. Then the child turned and buried her face in the seat.

Before Lydia could come up with a word, Simon appeared next to her. "Her name is Becky. She doesn't like to talk to strangers."

The words could have been said in

a variety of ways—excusing the child or expressing encouragement to her and thanks for Lydia's interest. Instead Simon made it sound as if she were at fault for intruding, and his disapproving expression forbade her from trying again.

The imp of mischief that never failed to lead her into something she shouldn't do suddenly came to life, and she responded with a cheerful smile.

"I just thought Becky might like to have a mug of hot chocolate to warm her up. I'm going to have one. What do you think, Becky?"

Simon's displeasure loomed over her, but she focused on the child, holding her hand out and smiling. For an instant she thought it was no good. But then a small hand found its way to hers, and she lifted the little girl to the ground. Hand in hand they headed for the door, and Lydia knew without looking that Simon was still frowning.

* * *

Simon watched them walk away, not sure whether he was pleased or annoyed. Of course he was happy to see his shy daughter willing to reach out to someone in what was a strange place to her, if not to him. But if she was ready to warm up to someone, did it have to be Lydia Stoltzfus?

He remembered Lydia. The pesky little kid next door, she'd been twice as much trouble as any of his younger siblings. She'd been an expert at leading the others into mischief, but she'd always come up smiling, no matter what. Everything had been a game to her.

Following them into Great-aunt Elizabeth's shop, he reminded himself that she was an adult now, but he wasn't quite convinced. Not when his first glimpse had been of her sprawled face down in the snow at the side of the road.

Aunt Elizabeth rushed to greet him, and he forgot Lydia in the warmth of her welcome. It had been too long, he thought. Too long since he'd been surrounded by people of his own blood, tied to him by unbreakable bonds of kinship. He and Rebecca had made good friends out west, but with her loss the longing had grown in him to return to Lost Creek, back where he could raise his daughter in the midst of family to love and care for them.

When he finally emerged from the hugs and exclamations, it was to find Becky installed at a table near the counter, with a mug of hot chocolate topped with whipped cream in front of her. With Lydia's help, she seemed to be trying to decide between a cruller and one of Aunt Elizabeth's cream horns.

"I think you'd like this one," he told her, pointing to the cream horn. "Aunt Bess fills the whole thing with yummy cream." His old name for his much-loved great-aunt came automatically to his lips.

Becky looked at him, then seemed

to look at Lydia for approval. When she smiled and nodded, Becky's hand clasped the cream horn, squirting out cream as she put it on her plate. She seemed confused for a moment, and then she carefully licked the cream off her fingers. Something in him eased at Becky's enjoyment, and his gaze met Lydia's for an instant of shared pleasure that startled him.

"Ach, this is our little Becky." Aunt Bess beamed down at the child. "Lydia is taking gut care of you, ain't so? She takes care of everybody, even me."

Before he could wrap his mind around this unexpected relationship between Aunt Bess and Lydia, the older woman surged on. "Lyddy, why don't you show Simon the extra storeroom? He's going to put some things there until his new house is ready."

Lydia, busily putting mugs of coffee on the table, looked up and nodded, while Simon's daad sat down next to Becky with every appearance of settling in for a bit. Before Simon quite knew what had happened, Lydia was leading him behind the counter to the cluster of rooms that made up the back of the building.

"I don't want to take you away from your work," he said. "This could wait."

Lydia shook her head. "Don't you remember? It's always best to listen to what Aunt Bess says. Otherwise she'll just keep after you and after you."

He couldn't help smiling at the accurate description of his great-aunt. "From what she said, it sounds as if she must listen to you. What did she mean about you taking care of her?"

"Ach, that's nothing." A flush that reminded him of peaches came up in Lydia's creamy cheeks. "She had a bad bout with pneumonia this winter, and since she insisted on staying in her apartment upstairs, everyone had to gang up on her to keep her out of the shop. That's all."

She opened one of the doors off the

kitchen. "Here's the room she was talking about. We didn't know what you might need, so I just cleaned it out and left it empty."

A quick glance told him there was more than enough space for the furniture and belongings he'd had shipped home. "Denke, Lydia." He felt a bit awkward, as if he'd lost his footing in trying to fit back into the life he'd left behind. "I wouldn't want to trouble you. I could have taken care of it."

"It's my job," she said simply, but there was a twinkle in the deep blue of her eyes that suggested she understood his discomfort.

There didn't seem to be anything else to say. "Denke," he repeated. This new, grown-up Lydia confused him. At moments she seemed to be a calm, poised stranger, and then he'd get a quick glimpse of that giddy, naughty child. He could only hope that everyone he met wouldn't be equally confusing.

He discovered he was not only returning her smile, he was appreciating the effect of eyes more deeply blue than the depths of a pond and the honey gold of her hair, whose tendrils, loose from her kapp, were drying in tiny curls.

Oh no. He backed off those thoughts abruptly, turning away so sharply that he feared it must look rude. Still, that was better than any alternative. He had lost Rebecca only a year ago, and he had no thoughts to spare for another woman, even if he had room in his heart. His goals were clear in front of him—to raise Becky among his own people, to build a home for them on Daad's farm, establish his clock-and watch-repair business so he could run it and look after Becky at the same time.

No, he had no time to spare for women. And especially not for one who still contained sparks of the frivolous, pesky child she'd been.

* * *

Lydia told herself she was just as happy when Simon returned abruptly to the table to sit with his family. After all, she had work to do. She didn't have time for a man who could look at her with obvious approval one minute and change to a glowering frown the next.

Still, she welcomed the sight of Frank Pierce, one of her regulars, coming in and stamping snow from his boots, his cheeks as red as apples and his white hair standing up in tufts when he pulled off his cap.

"Frank, what are you doing out on a snowy day like this? Doesn't your sister have any coffee for you at home?" She helped him off with the heavy winter jacket he wore. Frank lived with his equally elderly sister a block or two down Main Street, and his usual exercise was walking to the coffee shop every day to sit with several cronies and solve the world's problems.

"She's always telling him it'll stunt his growth," one of his buddies spoke up, making room for him.

"And she's not as pretty as our Lydia," another said, winking at her.

"Ach, you're all terrible, that's what you are." She gave him the answer she knew he expected, and went to get the coffeepot and another mug. They were all proud of themselves for braving the snow, she could tell, and if pretending to flirt with her made them happy, she was glad to oblige.

Unfortunately, someone didn't seem to agree. Lydia caught a definite scowl from Simon as she turned back from another round of refilling cups and chatting. She whisked behind the counter and pulled out a poster on which she was listing the week's specials. If Simon didn't approve of her, that was just too bad.

A moment later she was chiding herself for her unkind thought. Simon might have been frowning about something else entirely. The good Lord knew he'd plenty to worry about in his circumstances.

Bending over the poster, she was able to study him, thinking about how he'd changed from the boy she remembered. Not in coloring. His hair was still the deep brown of the buckeyes they used to find and shine, with dark brown eyes to match. Simon had always been quiet and serious—introverted, although she hadn't known the word at the time. He was the oldest, and took on all the responsibility that went with being the oldest son in a large Amish family.

Her thoughts flickered to her own brother. Josiah had certainly been very aware of what was expected of him, but no one could call him introverted. Or quiet. He was always only too likely to yell if he caught any of his younger siblings doing something he didn't think they should.

Maybe the truth was that Simon's early tendencies had just been intensified by grief and the responsibility for a motherless child. Those had carved the lines in his face that hadn't been there before and given his eyes the look of one carrying too heavy a burden.

Elizabeth looked up from the discussion and gestured to her, so Lydia seized the coffeepot and headed to their table. "More coffee? Hot chocolate?"

Enos slid his mug over for a refill. "Looks like the snow's about done. You shouldn't have any trouble getting home."

"That's good." She hadn't even noticed, but she looked now and saw that the snow on the street had already turned to wet slush.

"We were just talking about getting Simon's things into the storeroom, Lyddy. So if he comes when I'm upstairs, you'll know what to do. And we'd best find the key for that door so we can keep it locked."

Lydia nodded. "I know just where it is, but maybe I should have a duplicate made, so Simon can have his own."

"Whatever you think." Elizabeth sank back in the chair, and Lydia realized she was tiring. It had been this way ever since she was sick. She'd be talking and working like her old self, and then suddenly she'd be exhausted and need to lie down.

"I'll take care of it." Lydia glanced at Enos to see if he'd noticed, but he seemed oblivious, as did Simon. She paused behind Elizabeth's chair. "Isn't it about time for your rest?"

Elizabeth reached up to pat her hand. "In a minute. Why don't you see if there's something Becky can do? She's tired of listening to our talk."

That was like Elizabeth, ignoring her own difficulties to pay attention to someone else's. And she was right. Becky struck her as too well-behaved to wiggle, but she did look up hopefully at the suggestion.

"Sure thing." She held out her hand to the little girl again. "How about helping me make a poster?"

Becky shot a look at her father, maybe asking permission, and then she slid down and grasped her hand. Lydia took her to the counter where she'd been working on the list of specials and provided her with some colored pencils.

"Suppose you help me put some flowers around the edges so it will look like spring? And then I'll do the lettering in the middle. Okay?"

Becky looked carefully at the tulip Lydia was drawing, and then she nodded. Still without speaking, she started making a blue flower.

Was she always this quiet? With her hair so pale it was nearly white and her very light skin color, she resembled her mother the way Lydia remembered her. Every child was close to her mother, of course, and their resemblance might have made the bond even tighter. Perhaps she had inherited her father's quiet disposition, too, but even so, this seemed extreme.

"I like that flower. It's really pretty—just the color of your eyes."

That brought a startled look to Becky's face. "Really?" she said, as if she'd never thought of it.

"For sure. Your mammi had those bright blue eyes, too, I remember."

Abruptly she was aware of having said the wrong thing. The tiny face closed again. Becky slid down from the stool she was perched on and went silently back to her father. And although Becky didn't speak, she seemed to communicate with her father, because the look Simon shot at Lydia made her feel about six inches high.

If she could explain...

But she suspected that would only make matters worse. Probably she shouldn't have mentioned Becky's mother, but how would she know that? In any event, she didn't see Simon regarding her as anything but trouble. Probably the best thing she could do was to avoid both father and daughter as completely as possible, but that wasn't going to be easy.

Chapter Two

Determined to avoid any further misunderstandings with Simon, Lydia kept her mind on her work. Unfortunately, the café wasn't as busy as normal. The snow had discouraged shoppers, and now the melting slush looked equally messy underfoot. When she found herself starting back to the same table for the fourth time, she decided that pretending to be busy was harder work than actually being busy.

Another glance at Elizabeth left her feeling even more concerned. Elizabeth seemed to be staying upright through sheer force of will, and her gaze had become glassy with fatigue. Couldn't either of the men see it? Perhaps she should try again to persuade her...

A tug at her skirt interrupted Lydia's train of thought. Becky stood next to her, looking from her to the counter where the poster still lay unfinished. The sight of that tiny heart-shaped face struck her heart and melted it even faster than the sun melted the slush.

"Do you think we should finish the poster?" she asked.

Becky's nod was accompanied by a slight smile.

"Let's do it, then." She pulled a chair over so Becky could kneel on it next to the counter. "There, that should make it easier. Which color do you want next?"

Becky studied the colored pencils for a moment. Then her small finger pointed to the yellow one.

"Yellow it is," Lydia said. She put the pencil in the child's hand. "Yellow's a pretty color, isn't it? It reminds me that the daffodils will be coming out soon. Your grossmammi has them planted along the front of the porch, I know."

"She does?"

It was the closest Becky had come to continuing a conversation, and Lydia was delighted. "You ask her to show you where the daffodils are. I think you might find the green spears of the plants out of the ground already. You can check how they're growing, ain't so?"

Becky just nodded, but it was a companionable nod, as if they didn't need words between them.

Maybe Becky resembled her mother in looks, but certainly not in personality. From what she remembered of Rebecca, she had been always poised and in control of herself. Not outgoing, but friendly. Becky clearly took after her father in personality. She had the same grave, questioning attitude that Lydia remembered on Simon's face whenever he was confronted by something new. Funny how clear that image was in her mind.

Picking up a purple pencil, she added a row of the Dutch irises that fringed the creek near the old willow tree. But her mind was still busy with little Becky. How was such a shy, reserved child getting along in the crowded Fisher household? Enos and Mary had four children younger than Simon, and his next brother was married and lived there with his wife and baby. And all of them were cheerful, talkative and a bit overwhelming, she'd think, for Becky.

"I have to see if anyone wants more coffee," she told Becky. "Do you want to stay here until I get back?"

Becky looked from her to the poster, which had sprouted a whole row of what were probably meant to be daffodils. "Stay here," she said firmly.

"Gut." Lydia nodded, satisfied that Becky was feeling more at ease here.

Picking up the coffeepot, she moved from table to table, refilling cups.

She paused next to where Elizabeth sat with Simon and his father. She couldn't help it. She'd have to say something, even if she annoyed Elizabeth.

But even as she thought it, she caught Simon's eyes, and a message seemed to pass between them. He glanced toward his aunt and frowned slightly, clearly seeing what Lydia did.

"Becky, come along. And thank Lydia for letting you help her."

The child did so reluctantly, with a longing look at the poster, and gave Lydia a slight nod and a soft denke.

Nudging his daad's elbow, Simon got up.

"Time for us to be moving along," he said. "And time for Aunt Bess to have a rest, ain't so?"

"Ach, all of you fuss over me too much," Elizabeth said, but it was clear that fatigue dragged at her, and she tacitly admitted it, getting up slowly.

"Some people are worth fussing over," he replied, giving her a hug, his face softening so that he resembled the boy he'd been before sorrow had driven those lines of pain into his face. "Lyddy, you make sure she rests, yah?"

The old nickname, coupled with the reminder of the boy he once was, disoriented Lydia for a moment. Telling herself not to be so foolish, she nodded.

"I'll see to it. And I'll get Becky's coat." She'd hung it in the hallway to dry, so she hurried to take it from the peg and help Becky to put it on. The little girl paused to study the poster for a moment.

"It looks fine," Lydia assured her. "Next time you come, you'll see it right up there on the wall for everyone to look at."

Simon moved next to his daughter, helping her to fasten her coat and wrap a muffler securely around her neck. Meanwhile, Lydia gathered up a handful of colored pencils, making sure to include the yellow one, and put them in a bag.

She knelt next to Becky, very aware of Simon's strong figure standing next to her. "Here are some colored pencils for you to take home."

Becky's eyes grew wide, making her look even more like her mother. "For me?" she whispered.

"For you," Lydia said, touched. "Will you draw some more flowers?"

The child nodded, holding them close. "Yah, I will." Turning, she showed them to her daadi.

Simon cupped his daughter's face with his large hand, his smile very tender. "You'll make lots of them, ain't so?"

He turned the smile on Lydia then, and her heart seemed to grow warm in her chest. "Denke, Lyddy."

Usually the use of the nickname called

forth a correction. She was Lydia now. Not a child with a childish name. But it didn't seem to matter at all what Simon called her, not when he looked at her with the lines of pain eased in his face.

She nodded, unable to find any words. They headed for the door, and Lydia told herself firmly that she wouldn't stand there and watch them go. She put her arm around Elizabeth's waist.

"Rest time for you," she said, in a tone that didn't allow for argument. "Komm."

"You're a gut girl, Lyddy," Elizabeth murmured, patting her arm. "Gut for Simon and Becky, too, I see."

Firmly telling herself that she would not blush, she led Elizabeth toward the stairs.

Despite the slush that lingered, the buggy moved smoothly along the two-lane road as Simon drove home.

"Typical late March snow," Daad commented. "Feel the warmth of the sun.

The road will be dry by the time Lyddy heads home."

Simon nodded. Maybe this was a good time to get some questions answered. "I didn't realize Lydia was so close to Aunt Bess."

"Ach, yah, she's been as gut as a granddaughter to her. I don't know what we'd have done without her a couple of months back when Aunt Bess was so sick. She wouldn't listen to anybody, and wouldn't hear of us coming to stay, but Lyddy managed everything."

That was the impression he'd gotten from the conversation, and at one level it still seemed surprising to him. "I guess little Lyddy has grown up and left mischief behind."

Daad chuckled. "I wouldn't say that, exactly. She still likes to laugh, and she'll play with the young ones like she's their age. Well, you saw how she made friends with our little Becky."

"Yah, she did." And it looked as if he'd

have to refine his opinion of Lydia a bit. She might have been flirty with the customers, but she'd been good with Becky as well as taking care of Aunt Bess. It was quite a mixture.

Thinking of Becky, he glanced at the back seat. Becky had the bag open, but with her usual caution, she hadn't taken the pencils out in the buggy. But she'd put her hand in to finger them, smiling and relaxed. Yah, whatever her flaws, Lydia had been good with Becky. Still, that didn't mean he should encourage their relationship. Without Rebecca to help him, he had to be extra careful in raising their daughter.

When he turned into the farm lane, he naturally looked toward the site they'd decided on for his house and shop. Daad followed his gaze, shaking his head.

"All this wet isn't going to help in getting your house done, ain't so? We'll not get the foundation dug until it dries out, that's certain sure."

Simon nodded, fighting the depression that swept over him. His longing to have a place of their own had risen to a point where he could hardly think of anything else. He'd get out there with a shovel by himself if he thought it would do any good.

"Don't fret." Daad seemed to read his thoughts, and he put his hand on Simon's shoulder for a brief moment. "Once it's started, it will go up fast. And you know we love having you and little Becky living with us as long as you want."

"Denke," he murmured. He could hardly say that he and Becky were eager to get out, not when everyone was so happy that they were there.

But it was true. If he couldn't go back to the life he'd had with Rebecca, then he'd settle for just the two of them—him and Becky—in a home of their own.

Rebecca. His heart ached at the thought of going on without her beside him. It had been a great sorrow to both of them that there had been no more babies after Becky, but they had adjusted. The three of them had been contented, happy in their own home. Now he wanted, as best he could, to provide that again for Becky.

Daad meant it when he said they were welcome to live with them, but he knew, and he thought Daad was beginning to realize, that it wouldn't do.

When they walked into the kitchen a few minutes later, he was reminded all over again why it wouldn't do. The rest of the family had started lunch, and everyone seemed to be talking at once. They were hustled to the table with even more laughter and chatter, and Becky seemed to shrink against him.

"Denke." He resisted his brother Thomas's efforts to get Becky to sit between him and Sarah, his twin. "I think Becky wants to stay next to me for now."

"Sure thing." Thomas gave Becky a big smile. "Maybe next time." He was trying to understand, Simon thought, but it was obvious that he didn't. The entire family was outgoing, cheerful and noisy. He had always been the odd one, and he wondered sometimes where it had come from.

Rebecca had understood, and their home had been a haven of peace. Then the accident had robbed them—his mind cringed away from that. He couldn't think about it. He wouldn't.

Mammi leaned over to talk softly to Becky, and Daad began telling the story of finding Lyddy's buggy off the road. The twins, at fourteen eager to find humor in every mishap, promptly started talking about how they'd tease Lydia.

"You'd best be careful," Simon put in. "Or I might just have to tell her about the time you forgot to buckle the harness and the gelding trotted off without you and the buggy."

Thomas flushed, but he was laughing, always ready to take a good joke on himself. "No fair. I wasn't old enough to remember any of your mistakes."

"I am." His brother Adam looked up from the baby daughter he was bouncing on his knee. "Let's see what I can think of."

"If you don't mind how hard you're bouncing, the boppli is going to spit up her lunch all over you." Adam's wife, Anna Mae, swooped down on him and rescued her small daughter. "Komm, now. Get finished and back to work so Simon and Becky can have their lunch in peace."

Peace. That was what Becky needed. He'd grown up in this house, with all his noisy younger siblings, and he'd survived all right. Why not? It had been that way ever since he could remember.

But Becky hadn't. Instead she'd been plunged into it while still in the midst of her grief over losing her mother. Naturally, she was finding it hard to cope.

They meant well. He couldn't doubt that. The twins were old enough to feel responsible for their little niece, and they wanted to love her and help her. It wasn't their fault that Becky was so easily overwhelmed. He couldn't ask them to change their ways in their own home. If only he and Becky had someplace else to stay. Then Becky could get acquainted with them more gradually, learning to join in the fun, he hoped.

But finding another place to stay was impossible. Mammi had taken it hard enough when she'd learned he planned to build a house of his own for himself and Becky. Oh, she'd never dream of saying so, but he knew she longed to have them both right here under her wing. The idea that they'd stay someplace other than the family home until their place was ready—well, she couldn't possibly understand, and she'd be hurt.

Somehow they had to make it through this. His gaze rested on Becky. Somehow.

* * *

By the time the coffee shop closed at four, Lydia had already done most of the cleanup. Once the snow had melted from the sidewalks, she was briefly busy again, but that had ebbed as the afternoon wore on. Now she could set off for home.

Elizabeth was coming out of the storeroom Lydia had emptied for Simon's belongings. Lydia glanced inside but saw nothing different. "Is something wrong?"

"Ach, no." Elizabeth patted her cheek. "You go on home now, Lyddy. I'll lock up."

Lydia took a closer look at her elderly employer. The fatigue seemed to be hanging on for a long time. "Are you sure?"

"Positive." Elizabeth made shooing motions. "Go. And thank you for being so sweet with little Becky. That poor child needs all the love and kindness she can get."

Lydia nodded, her eyes stinging at the thought of losing a mother so young. "If I know the Fisher family, she'll be overwhelmed by it."

"Yah." Elizabeth looked thoughtful. "Maybe...well, never mind. I'll see you tomorrow."

As she drove out of town, Lydia was still wondering what had been on Elizabeth's mind. Perhaps she was thinking, as Lydia herself was, that a shy child like Becky needed careful handling. Simon, seeming consumed by his own grief, might not be the best judge of how exactly to give her that.

It wasn't her business, she told herself firmly. Except in so far as they were neighbors and part of the church family, anyway. If she could do something for them, she would, but Simon hadn't looked as if he would welcome her interference.

The day's unexpected snow had melted from the road as if it had never been. Only a rut in the side of the road was left to show where she'd slid off, and already the sun felt warm. Small patches of bright green showed here and there—onion grass, she supposed. That was early spring in central Pennsylvania. Or late winter. Unpredictable, but even under the snow, spring was waiting.

When she walked into the kitchen a few minutes later, Mammi looked pleased.

"Just in time. I have some laundry to go over to the daadi haus for your grossmammi. You can take it."

"Yah, sure." Lydia hung up her bonnet and reached for the basket, but her brother Josiah got there first.

"Not until we hear all about it," he said, teasing.

"All about what?" She tried to look innocent, knowing she'd have to endure some kidding about her misadventure.

"The accident? You know. Going right off the road and needing Enos to rescue you?"

"Was ist letz?" Mammi was instantly alert. Apparently, Josiah hadn't blabbed to her.

"Nothing, Mammi. The right-side wheels slid off the road a little when that snow hit. I'd have persuaded Dolly to pull back on even if Enos hadn't come along."

"So you say." Josiah wasn't done teasing.

Daad frowned, setting down the coffee mug that was always in his hand when he wasn't working. "How did you come to do that, daughter? Dolly is usually sure-footed."

"It wasn't Dolly's fault. A car came up behind us way too fast, shoving us right off the edge."

Mammi shivered a little, touching

Lydia's shoulder as if to make sure she was still there. "Those cars go too fast."

"Especially when it's snowing," Josiah added, handing her the basket.

"Give me a horse every time," Daad said. "Animals have instincts. Cars don't." He picked up his coffee mug, apparently feeling he'd said it all.

"Right." Lydia seized the basket and headed toward the daadi haus before anyone could mention Simon and start asking questions.

Of course, when she reached the daadi haus, she'd have to avoid Grossmammi's sharp eyes, and no one ever succeeded in doing that. She and her cousins used to think her grandmother could see right through them, and Lydia still wasn't sure about that.

Sure enough, Grossmammi took one look at her and gestured to a chair at the small round table in her kitchen. "Komm, sit, and we'll have tea. You can tell me about Simon Fisher."

Sighing, Lydia put the basket down. No one ever evaded Grossmammi for long. And there was no one else she'd rather talk to anyway.

"There's not much to tell," she said. "He's back with his little girl, and he's planning to settle here."

Grossmammi put two mugs of tea on the table and sat down next to her. "Poor boy. How does he look?"

She considered, stirring sugar into her tea. "Older. Much older. Losing Rebecca has aged him. I hardly knew what to say."

Grossmammi clucked softly. "Poor boy," she said again. "It's never easy to lose a spouse, no matter the circumstances. And Rebecca was so young."

Lydia could only nod, because her throat choked at the thought. She swallowed hard and found her voice.

"I suppose he never imagined such a thing. Now with the little girl to raise, it will be so hard for both of them." Lydia took a gulp of the hot tea. Mint, this time. Grossmammi grew her own herbs and made her own tea, and she knew mint was Lydia's favorite.

"Tell me about the child. She's called after her mammi, I remember."

"Yah, but he calls her Becky. She seems small for her age, and she's very fair."

"Just like Rebecca," Grossmammi commented. She had an encyclopedic memory when it came to every member of the Leit, as well as their families going back several generations.

"She is the image of Rebecca," Lydia said slowly, remembering the child's reaction. "But she acted very odd when I mentioned that she had eyes like her mammi. She just…" Lydia spread her hands, palms up. "She closed down. That's all I can call it. We had been coloring together, and she put down her pencil and went straight back to her daadi." She didn't add that Simon had given her an angry look. Grossmammi didn't need to know that.

"Poor, poor child," Grossmammi crooned sadly. "She needs lots of loving. Still, I'm sure she'll get that if I know the Fisher family."

Lydia nodded, but she wondered. How was that shy little girl going to react to the rest of the noisy, outgoing Fisher clan, no matter how loving?

She didn't realize how long she'd been silent, musing about it, until her grandmother clasped her hand. "Is it making you sad, then, seeing Simon again like this?"

For a moment she didn't know how to respond. Just as Grossmammi seemed to be able to read her thoughts, so she could tell what her grandmother had in mind.

"For sure. It would make anyone sad, ain't so?" Feeling Grossmammi continue to study her, she had to go on. "If you're thinking that I had a crush on

Simon once, forget it. I was nothing but a child then. I'm all grown up, and I don't get crushes any longer."

"You always have a soft spot for the first person you loved, no matter how impossible it was. But it's not impossible now. Simon ought to remarry. Not right away, but soon enough to give his daughter a mammi."

"Don't look at me," Lydia said emphatically, hoping to ward off any matchmaking. "I'm not looking for a husband. And I don't think I ever will be. Somebody has to be the maidal aunt. Why not me?"

Her grandmother shook her head slowly. "Are you still fretting about Thomas Burkhalter? It wasn't your fault."

The name was like a knife in her soul. "Of course not." Lydia kept her voice firm and tried not to show what she felt. "That would be foolish."

But foolish or not, it was true, and she

suspected Grossmammi knew it as well as she did. What happened to Thomas— She backed away from the memory and slammed the door on it. She would not start remembering. She wouldn't.

"I just wondered," Grossmammi said, her voice mild. "As for the little girl, it sounds as if you made friends with her, at least, if you were coloring with her."

Lydia nodded, grabbing at the change of subject. "She needs friends, that's certain sure."

"Maybe that's why the gut Lord put her right in your path, Lydia. He may mean for you to help that child, so don't you miss the chance."

"I'll try not to." She knew Grossmammi's teachings about not ignoring the jobs the Lord put in front of you. But she suspected that Simon wouldn't be eager to see her doing anything with his daughter.

Chapter Three

True to the fickle weather, the next day was a delicious taste of spring. The sun shone, the onion grass and dandelion greens looked ready to be plucked, and spring bulbs sent green spears reaching heavenward.

Lydia smiled as she arrived in town. She could look ahead to a busy morning, given how many people were out on the street already. A cluster of children skipped and hopped along the walk to the elementary school, and an elderly woman stepped out of her door and tilted her face toward the sun, looking as if she'd emerged from a long winter's nap.

Sure enough, no sooner had she turned the sign on the door to Open than the bell jingled. Frank and his buddy Albert burst in laughing. "We're first," Frank announced, grinning at Lydia. "Keep the coffee coming."

Albert waved the weekly newspaper in one hand, which meant for sure that they'd have plenty to talk about. The paper might only come out once a week, but it was crammed with the sort of news that they liked best, since it was all about their neighbors.

Lydia exchanged amused glances with Elizabeth and seized the coffeepot. "They've got spring fever, yah?"

"I don't doubt it." Elizabeth shook her head as she pulled out a tray of cream horns. "Naomi hasn't come by with the shoofly pies yet, so they'll have to start on something else."

Nodding, Lydia hurried to take care

of her favorite customers. Several of their Amish neighbors supplied the coffee shop with fresh-baked treats, which gave them an extra source of income while also making it unnecessary for Elizabeth to spend so much of her time baking.

She'd pushed Elizabeth into letting her set up the arrangement with the women when Elizabeth had been so ill, and she just hoped it would continue. Elizabeth had enough drive for a woman half her age, but she'd begun to look frail, and Lydia feared for her health.

Scurrying back and forth, keeping customers happy, Lydia was relieved to see Naomi Schutz rush in carrying her usual boxes of shoofly pies. Naomi began unpacking them, and after a quick glance at the crowded room, started cutting and serving without waiting to be asked.

"Denke," Lydia murmured to her in

passing, with a cautious glance toward Elizabeth.

"I was late, so I'll stay and help for a bit. It won't hurt James to listen for the baby this morning." With only one child left at home, Naomi seemed to be enjoying her time out, and Lydia nodded her thanks.

In another hour, the rush was over. Lydia had just persuaded Elizabeth to sit down with a cup of coffee when someone banged at the back door.

"I'll get it." She pressed the woman back in her chair. "Must be a delivery."

It was a delivery, all right, but not anything she expected. Instead, a moving van had pulled up by the door, and a burly man in jeans and a T-shirt leaned against the door.

"Furniture for Simon Fisher," he declared, waving a paper in one hand.

"That's right." She stood back, holding the door wide. "Come in and I'll show you where it goes."

He kept shaking his head as she led him through the kitchen. "We thought we were supposed to be stacking it inside the door, not traipsing through a business."

Elizabeth had joined them by that time, and she looked upset. "But you can't do that. How would we get through? The furniture…"

Lydia put her arm around Elizabeth. "It's all right. You go and leave a message at the farm for Simon. I'll show them where to put the things."

Elizabeth fussed for another minute while storm clouds gathered on the man's face, but Lydia finally convinced her. As she trotted off to the phone, Lydia turned to the man.

"Come, now. You know you're supposed to put things where I want them."

"You're not Simon Fisher." He made what she hoped was a final objection.

"I'm acting for him," she said firmly. "You stack everything in the storeroom, and I'll get coffee and shoofly pie ready for you and your crew."

He considered for another moment and then gave in. "All right," he grumbled. "It better be good."

"Freshly baked this morning," she assured him, wondering why some people had to make a fuss before getting on with things.

Once the decision was made, they worked quickly. Boxes, trunks, tables and chairs all began to make their way through the kitchen, while she kept the way clear for them.

As the parade dwindled down, Lydia followed them into the storeroom, hoping everything had made it safely. Things were stacked in a helter-skelter fashion, but at least they were all upright and in one piece. She winced when she saw a hand-painted dower chest dropped on top of an oak table, but a look at the man's face convinced her that further argument wouldn't help.

Besides, since Simon wasn't here, she couldn't very well sort things out. No doubt there were some things he'd want to unpack right away, but she didn't have any idea what. She'd just have to help him rearrange when he got here.

But when a barrel of dishes nearly fell off a dresser, she grabbed for it, letting her annoyance show. "That's breakable. Set it on the floor in the corner."

"Yeah, okay. Sorry." Fortunately, it was a younger man she was addressing now, hardly more than a boy, with a thin face and long hair straggling over his shoulders.

"Finish up now, and I'll fix you something to eat," she said after another look. "Okay?"

"Yes, ma'am." This time she got a smile, and he moved a little more quickly.

In another half hour the job was finished, and the workmen were clustered around one of the larger tables, drinking coffee and eating baked goods so fast it seemed there'd be nothing left for the customers. Before they could eat everything in sight the foreman seemed to recall another job, and he hustled them out.

Lydia exchanged glances with Elizabeth. "Not the best job I've ever seen, but at least everything is in."

"I'll just see if I should rearrange..." Elizabeth began, but Lydia shook her head, diverting her away from the storeroom.

"There's no point until Simon sorts through it himself. I'll take care of it later."

Elizabeth didn't look entirely convinced, but the sound of a buggy pulling into the alley distracted her. In another moment Simon and Becky came in from the side door.

"Our furniture is here?" He looked... torn, Lydia decided. As if he didn't know whether he wanted to see those remnants of his previous life again or not.

She could understand. Probably everything in the room would remind him of the happiness he used to have.

At her nod, Simon stalked toward the storeroom while Elizabeth busied herself with helping Becky and admiring the stuffed doll the child clutched. That left Lydia to deal with Becky's father, so she trailed after him.

They had hardly both gotten into the room before he rounded on her, anger replacing any other feelings. "What's happened in here? Did you let them just throw things in? Couldn't you have taken a little more care than that?"

Lydia tried to remind herself that this was difficult for him and struggled to keep her voice calm. "I thought you'd want to sort things out yourself before stacking them for storage. You weren't here when they came, remember?"

* * *

Simon saw the stricken look on Lydia's face the instant the words were out of his mouth. He barely had time to recognize it before Lydia was responding calmly. Young Lyddy had learned to control her temper, it seemed, while he...well, he'd discovered a temper he hadn't known he had.

From childhood, Lyddy had had the sort of temper that flared up quickly and was as quickly over. He hoped the fact that she could now hold it in check didn't mean she'd hold a grudge.

"I'm sorry," he muttered, feeling small in comparison. "That wasn't fair of me."

"Forget it." Lydia's smile said she had already done so. "I'm sure there are things you'll want to get out right away, and we can put the rest back against the wall. Where shall we start?"

He couldn't very well say that he didn't want help. He'd been rude enough for one morning. The truth was that he shrunk from unpacking boxes filled with memories.

"You have your own work to do. I can handle this."

Lydia smiled as if she'd expected that response. "We're not busy right now. And if I go out, you know that your aunt Bess will come in."

Frowning, Simon glared at her. The look didn't disturb her smile.

"Well?" She lifted her eyebrows in a question.

He forced himself to nod, even if he couldn't manage a smile. "Right. Denke. Becky wants some of her books and the clothes her mother made for her doll. And I'd like to find my tools. They're somewhere in this mess."

Looking around a little helplessly, he realized what a state he'd been in when he'd packed. Once the decision had been made, he'd been so eager to leave that he hadn't taken much time over packing. Their friends had all pitched in, of course, and he had no idea what they'd put where.

"I guess we'd best start opening boxes, then. I'll get something to cut the tape with."

Her brief absence was enough time for him to give himself a talking-to. He had to stop reacting so stiffly to people who were trying to help. He knew well that folks here would be just as eager to do something as their friends out West. They'd understand and forgive his rudeness, but he'd have trouble forgiving himself.

Lydia came back with a box cutter and a pair of long scissors, and her eyes twinkled with amusement.

"What?" he asked.

"You should see them with their heads together over cups of hot chocolate. Elizabeth is telling Becky a story, and you know what a storyteller she is—she almost acts it out while she talks."

He chuckled. "I remember. It's her gift, ain't so?"

Lydia nodded, laughing a little. "Now she has a new little one to listen to all of them. You've made her very happy."

"I hope." Suddenly whatever strain had been between them was gone, and he was talking to her as if she were the little neighbor he'd known since she was born. "Let's get on with it. I don't want Aunt Bess to have any excuse for trying to work in here."

They started opening boxes. Lydia worked methodically, checking the contents, asking if he wanted them now, and then marking each box before pushing it back against the wall. Simon realized he was grateful for her detached attitude. He tried to follow her lead.

He found he was watching her, liking the way she approached the job and her calm acceptance of the fact that he needed help. She would for anyone, he guessed. Little Lyddy had grown into a very competent young woman.

How was it that she wasn't married? She must be in her midtwenties by now, and she certain sure was appealing. The boys around here must not have any taste if they ignored her.

"I think I've found your tools," she announced.

Simon dropped what he was doing to move to her side, grasped the box and tore it the rest of the way open with an eagerness he hadn't felt in a while. "Right." He lifted out a caddy loaded with tools and then found the box that contained the smallest, finest tools he used on intricate clock repairs. Opening it on the spot, he took them out one at a time, making sure everything was there and none had been damaged.

"You look like a child at Christmas," Lydia observed, and he had to laugh.

"I feel like it, too. There's nothing

I'd rather do just now than get back to work."

She looked at him, seeming to consider his words. "Can't you? I mean, I know your house isn't built yet, but clock repair doesn't take a lot of space, does it? Maybe you could get started in a small way."

"Maybe I could." Reality asserted itself. "But not at home. The boys would be trying to borrow my tools, and Mammi would interrupt every five minutes to see if I wanted something to eat."

She chuckled at his words. "Ach, that's how a mother says she loves you, ain't so?"

Nodding, he put all of his repair tools back into a box and set it closer to the door. At least it would be there if he could figure out a way to get started.

"I guess you would need a little peace and quiet to do such detailed work," Lydia commented, replacing some sheets back in a box and labeling it. "I glad I don't have that sort of job. I'd rather have folks around while I'm working."

"Like those old guys who flirt with you?" He couldn't seem to keep a little tartness from his voice.

But Lydia shrugged it off. "It doesn't mean anything, and it makes them happy," she said placidly.

He almost didn't hear her, because he was too intent on the piece of furniture she'd just pulled into the light.

"Don't," he said sharply. But uselessly. Of course it had to come out, bringing the memories with it.

He stood next to her, reaching out to touch it with reluctant fingers, as if it would burn him.

It didn't, of course. It was just a piece of furniture, that was all. No matter what memories were attached to it.

"I'm sorry." Her voice was soft. "It's something special."

"Yah." For a moment he stood there,

silent, letting his hands run over the smooth wood of the rocker, as warm as if it were alive.

The momentary rebellion at the sight of it faded away, and he experienced a longing to talk—to say something to a listener who didn't share his grief.

"I made it for Rebecca when she was expecting Becky." With love in every step of it, he told himself. "She laughed, telling me to make it sturdy enough to last through a big family." His throat tightened. "It wasn't to be."

"It's hard to understand the Lord's will sometimes." Lyddy put her hand lightly on his arm, a featherlike touch that spoke of caring.

"Yah. It is." He put his hand over hers, turning to her to thank her for understanding. But the words didn't get said. They just stood there, inches apart, hands touching. And time seemed suspended. "Lyddy." He murmured her name. This was a new Lyddy, it seemed, with all the laughter and liveliness of the child added to a woman's softness and caring.

He thought...

Whatever it was, it was lost in the opening of the door and Aunt Bess's cheerful voice. He yanked his hand back and sensed Lyddy turn away. She was trying to put space between them, and he couldn't blame her.

Aunt Bess was asking him a question, and Becky was peeping cautiously into a box, her doll held against her. With a fierce effort, he turned to them, forcing himself to listen. Forcing himself not to show the mortification he felt.

He must never do that again. Never. He had found love once, and it had been taken away. He wouldn't look for it again, ever.

Lydia went straight to the kitchen, where she leaned against the sink and tried to catch her breath. Her cheeks felt as if they were on fire. She couldn't let anyone see her until she had control of herself, but she should be serving customers. Elizabeth would think she'd taken leave of her senses.

Come to think of it, maybe that wasn't so far wrong. Sucking in a breath, she bent over the sink and splashed some cold water on her face. There, that was better.

Lydia straightened, running her cold hand across the back of her neck. She had been caught off guard when the unthinkable happened, but she could control herself. But she'd never experienced anything like the feeling that overwhelmed her when she'd been so close and looked into Simon's eyes.

This was foolish. She was a grown woman, not a giddy teenager. She could keep her feelings in check. Still, it might be safer to stay clear of Simon as best she could.

Her grossmammi's voice sounded in

her head at that. *God puts people in our path because He expects us to help them.* That was what Grossmammi believed. If that grieving little family had been placed by God in her path, it wasn't right to run away from her responsibility.

Before she could argue with herself, she heard voices, and all three of them came out of the storeroom just as Lydia reached the counter. To be exact, Elizabeth was doing most of the talking. She seemed even more delighted than Simon and Becky over the arrival of their belongings. Maybe that made it more certain in her mind that Simon and Becky were here to stay.

Lydia smiled, watching them. Elizabeth would never admit to having favorites among her many great-nieces and nephews, but Lydia knew from the way she talked that Simon had a special place in her heart—maybe just because he was so different from his siblings.

Becky, clutching something to her chest along with her doll, trotted over to Lydia. "Look." She held out a little bundle of clothes.

She took them, spreading them on the counter and smoothing them out with her hand. Doll clothes, handmade for a typical Amish faceless doll. Every little girl had one, and although there might be other dolls, this one was usually the much-loved favorite. Lydia still had hers, tucked away in a dower chest her grandfather had made for her.

"They are so pretty." She held up a dress made from a bit of dark green fabric. The stitches were so tiny as to be almost invisible. "I think your doll must love this one."

Becky nodded solemnly. Then she looked through the rest, her face clouding as she looked a second time.

"Was ist letz? What's wrong?" She hated seeing the child's smile vanish.

"Her nightgown isn't here." Becky's

eyes filled with tears. "I was certain sure it would be. Daadi said it must be."

She could imagine it without any difficulty—the rush of getting ready to leave, trying to get all their household belongings packed up when they were already stressed and grieving. How easily something could go astray.

Lydia knelt beside her, blotting the tears with a napkin. "You know what? I have my doll and her clothes at home, and I'm sure she has a nightgown you can have. All right?"

Becky's face cleared a little, but not entirely. "But then your dolly wouldn't have a nightgown to sleep in."

"That's all right," Lydia said hastily. "I know she has an extra one, and we'd love to share. I'll get it out and bring it over as soon as I get home."

"For sure?" Her eyes lit up.

"For sure," Lydia echoed, smiling. It wasn't hard to help Becky. Helping her father would be a much more difficult, maybe impossible, task.

Elizabeth hurried over to grasp some coffee cups. "What's for sure? Are you two planning something?"

"The nightgown for Becky's doll is misplaced, so I'm going to get out the one—the extra one—I have. She'll want to have it by bedtime."

"Sehr gut," Elizabeth said approvingly. "Will you bring some doughnuts to the table? Simon wants a snack before he goes back to his sorting."

"You mean you insisted I have a snack," Simon said, looking himself again but avoiding Lydia's gaze. He took the coffee cups from his aunt and carried them to the nearest table, while Lydia brought a plate of doughnuts.

"Hot chocolate for Becky?" she asked, evading his eyes.

"Maybe a glass of milk instead. Denke, Lyddy."

She went for the milk, feeling slightly

better at hearing the nickname on his lips again.

When she returned, she caught the end of something Elizabeth was saying. "… don't see why not. It's the best solution."

Simon was shaking his head. "I don't think—"

"Ach, that's just because you think it would be a trouble for us, but it's not." Elizabeth was at her most determined, and when she set her mind on something, most folks just gave in, knowing she wouldn't let up until she was satisfied. Never something for herself, mind. Always something she thought best for others.

Lydia set the milk down in front of Becky and popped a straw in it. Becky's eyes widened, and she gave Lydia a whole-hearted smile, cradling her doll to her chest.

"Denke, Lyddy," she whispered.

Her heart expanding, Lydia nodded. Becky was opening up.

"Don't you agree with me, Lydia?" Elizabeth demanded.

She looked at them, trying to switch mental tracks. "Agree? I might, if I knew what you were talking about."

Elizabeth heaved a sigh. "Simon was showing me his tools. Didn't he show you, as well?"

"Yah," she said cautiously, wondering where this was going.

"It's obvious. Simon wants to get started on his business as fast as possible, and the ground is so wet that who knows when they'll be able to start on his house. So I think he should set up in the storeroom." She switched to Simon abruptly. "You said you had some work already in hand, and no place to do it. The storeroom is perfect—well, not perfect, but there's room, and we can bring in a table and extra lighting."

"I'm sure we could," Simon said, his patience stretching. "But I don't think it's a gut idea. It'll mean extra work for you and Lyddy, and…"

"That's ferhoodled, and you know it. It won't bother us to have you working in the other room. We won't even know you're there."

Lydia didn't know about Elizabeth, but she certain sure would be aware if Simon were in the next room. And she could see he was running out of excuses.

"You're forgetting about Becky." His face softened, and he touched his daughter's head lightly. "She wouldn't be happy at the farm without me all day. Not yet, anyway."

"So you'll bring her along whenever you want," his aunt replied. "She's a quiet child, and she'll be no trouble at all. She can even help, can't you, Becky?"

Becky's eyes, darting from one to another, settled on Elizabeth, and she nodded.

Elizabeth turned to Lydia, as she'd

known she would, and her thoughts whirled.

"You agree, don't you, Lyddy?"

If Elizabeth was going to start calling her Lyddy, the battle against the nickname was lost. And as for having them here, with Simon in and out every day, intruding into her thoughts and unsettling her emotions—well, any opposition was lost there, too. She couldn't look at Becky and say she didn't want them there, no matter how much she wanted to retreat.

"Yah, I do. I think it's a fine idea." She managed to look at Simon and smile, hoping her thoughts didn't show. Or her feelings.

Simon gave her a serious, measuring look, as if he were trying to see through her to the contents of her heart. Finally he nodded.

"I guess we may as well try it. Denke."

Were his reasons for reluctance the same as hers? She couldn't believe he felt anything for her. That was impossible, for a reason that anyone could see. He was still in love with his wife.

Chapter Four

A flurry of customers distracted Lydia and kept her busy for the next hour. But she couldn't help being aware of Simon and Becky's presence. Somehow it upset the balance of the shop, and she couldn't quite figure out why. Anyway, she just worked here. The important thing was that Elizabeth seemed happy and satisfied with this turn of events.

Becky stayed in the storeroom for a time, coming out now and then to put things in a box to be taken home with them. Lydia couldn't help smiling when she glanced at the child. Becky was entirely engrossed, and she'd lost the worried look that was too old for her little face.

Eventually, Becky seemed to tire of the activity. She came to Lydia and stood there, looking at her.

"Can I get something for you, Becky?" The earlier rush was over, and she had time now to concentrate on other things.

"Do you have some more paper I can use? Please?"

"For sure," she said, delighted that the child had come to her and asked for what she wanted. "Here's a table right here." She pointed to one near the wall, and Becky climbed onto a chair while Lydia got out paper placemats for coloring and a batch of the colored pencils.

She put one of the placemats in front of Becky and stacked the others. "There. That way you can make a lot of pictures, yah?"

Becky nodded and picked out a red

pencil. "I'll make some tulips for you and Aunt Bess."

"Wonderful gut! We'll like that."

She stepped back, her gaze meeting that of her employer. Elizabeth was smiling, and she touched her chest lightly. "She's stealing your heart, ain't so?" she murmured.

Lydia could only nod. "I can't resist her, I guess."

Elizabeth's smiled broadened, and she studied Lydia's face as if she'd been struck by an idea. But whatever it was, she didn't say anything, and Lydia turned away as the bell over the door tinkled.

Pleasure rushed through her when she saw her cousin. Beth was not only a cousin, she was a dear friend, and just the sight of her warmed Lydia's heart. The black dress she wore was a reminder that Beth had lost her husband last fall, but after a time of grief and pain at the revelation of his misdeeds, Beth seemed to have come through that dark night. Glancing at her sweet face, anyone could tell she'd regained her spirit. And if Lydia knew what was going on, Beth was well on the way to a lasting love.

Beth's son, five-year-old Noah, came in her wake, carefully wiping his shoes on the mat. Then he looked toward Lydia and grinned, blue eyes sparkling. "We came to see you," he announced.

"So I see." She gave him a quick hug. "I'm wonderful glad you did."

"We were shopping." Beth announced the obvious, putting a large paper bag on the floor near the coat hooks.

"Don't tell me you needed something you don't carry in your own store," she teased. Beth and Daniel Miller, her late husband's partner, ran a general merchandise store on the edge of town, and Noah was a proud helper there.

"Fabric and yarn," Beth said, showing her the contents of the bag. "I need to do a little sewing."

Lydia wondered if the deep purple fabric was meant for a dress that would mark the end of Beth's mourning clothes but thought it better not to ask. She and Beth and Miriam, their other girl cousin, told each other most everything, but this place was too public for a serious conversation.

"I heard that Simon Fisher is here. He's back to stay, ain't so?" Beth gave her a quick hug once she'd hung up their jackets. "That's gut news."

"Yah, it is." She glanced toward the storeroom, but Simon wasn't in sight. "He's back in the storeroom now, but you'll probably see him before you leave. And this is his daughter, Becky." She led them to the table where Becky was ensconced. "Becky, this is my cousin Beth, and her boy, Noah. He's about the same age as you. That means you'll both start school in September."

"Hi, Becky. What are you doing? Making a picture?" Noah leaned on the chair across from her.

Becky stared at him shyly, and Lydia hoped she'd respond. She didn't speak, but after a moment she shoved a paper placemat and a handful of pencils toward him.

Apparently, Noah recognized that as an invitation, and he climbed on the chair and seized a colored pencil.

"That's fine," Beth said. "You color, and then you can have a treat later. Cousin Lyddy and I want to talk."

"Your timing was perfect." Lydia said, leading her to a nearby table. "We've been busy off and on all day, but it should be fairly quiet now. Coffee?"

"What about some of Grossmammi's herbal tea?" Beth took a packet from her bag and handed it to Lydia. "For you."

"You didn't have to bring it," she protested. "You should know we have a wonderful supply at our house."

"I know, but I thought some spearmint would taste right, and you might not have it here."

"You're getting as bad as Grossmammi," Lydia teased, taking the packet. "A special herb for every season. Spearmint for spring, yah?"

"Yah, and who knows why? It's Grossmammi's secret."

Still smiling, Lydia went to bring the kettle to a boil and warm the teapot. Seeing Beth always made her feel better, not that she'd needed cheering up. They'd been constantly together when they were kinder, but growing up had changed some things. Not their friendship, though, no matter how many times they saw each other.

When she returned with the brewed tea, Beth was smiling in the direction of Becky and Noah. "She's a child of few words, ain't so?"

"Shy, that's all." Lydia grew more serious. "This hasn't been easy. Losing her mammi and now trying to get used to a new place and new people."

"Kinder do adapt," Beth said gently, a touch of wistfulness in her voice. And she should know, having her own fatherless child. But Noah had Daniel, who seemed to be doing a wonderful gut job of being just what they both needed.

Brushing away her momentary sadness, Beth pulled something else from her bag and handed it to Lydia. "A letter from Miriam," she said, referring to their cousin. "She says she's coming home soon, and she sounds excited about it."

"We're be sehr happy to have her back." Lydia seized the letter and tucked it away for later reading and answering. Their round-robin letters had kept the three of them close while they were apart. She was about to say something else about Miriam when Elizabeth, coming down from a short rest, saw Beth and exclaimed happily.

In another moment the two of them were chatting, and Lydia fetched another cup, then moved to the children's table to check on Becky and Noah.

Noah showed her his picture. "I made a really big daisy."

She might not have been positive without his identification, since the daisy seemed to have purple spots. "Very colorful," she said tactfully.

"My picture is big, too." Becky's voice was soft, but she seemed determined not to be outdone, which Lydia considered a good sign.

"I like that one, too."

"Mine's brighter." Noah frowned. As an only child, he wasn't used to competition.

Becky's lip trembled, and Lydia realized a quick intervention was needed. "I'll show you something else you can do with a flower picture." Grabbing an extra sheet, she sketched a quick flower with an orange pencil, and then made two holes in the center.

"You'll ruin it," Noah said.

"No, I won't." She held it up to her face, peering through the small holes. "I made it into a mask, so I can pretend to be a flower."

She made the flower sway from side to side, as if it moved in the breeze.

Noah clapped. "Show Mammi. I want one, too. Look, Mammi." He grabbed her hand, trying to swing her around.

Lydia swung, the mask slipped, and she couldn't see a thing.

"Whoa." She broke up in laughter. "You're going to pull the flower right out of the ground."

"I'll help you." Becky actually said it loud enough to be heard, and she jumped from her chair to catch hold of Lydia's skirt.

Laughing with sheer joy at Becky joining in, Lydia caught hold of her hand

and swung her and Noah around until they were all laughing.

Except for one person. Simon had come out of the storeroom, and laughter was the last thing on his face.

For a moment no one spoke, and it must have been as obvious to Elizabeth and Beth that Simon wasn't pleased about her.

"There you are, Simon." Elizabeth sounded deliberately cheerful. "Komm, join the fun. Lyddy is helping Becky get to know a new playmate."

His expression cleared, but not without some effort. "So I see. Who is this young man?"

"That's my boy, Noah." Beth rose to greet him. "You remember me, yah?"

"For sure. It's gut to see you, Beth."

Lydia realized he was trying to sound friendly, but it was a shame that he had to try so hard. Couldn't he see that everyone here wanted the best for him and Becky?

She handed the improvised mask to Becky. The child smiled, looked through it, and then handed it to Noah, a gesture that warmed Lydia's heart. If Becky could open up, even a little, it was surely the best thing for both father and daughter. Maybe he'd be able to follow her example, and Lydia prayed it might be so.

Simon found it impossible to relax, even when he was well on his way back to the farm. He'd longed to return to Lost Creek, and for the most part he was pleased to be here. But being around people who'd known you all your life had disadvantages, too. They felt only too free to meddle.

He glanced at Becky, snuggled up next to him on the buggy seat. If she hadn't wanted to leave the coffee shop, she hadn't complained, either. Had she really enjoyed the silly playacting that seemed to erupt when Lyddy was around?

Chiding himself for being unfair,

he shook his head. He shouldn't criticize Lyddy, even in his own mind. She must have many good qualities, or Aunt Bess wouldn't be so fond of her. Still, he wasn't sure she was the best person to have around his Becky.

Such a good child. He put his arm around her, and she looked up at him with a sweet smile that almost brought tears to his eyes. He was the one who knew his daughter best, he assured himself.

She was very quiet, he admitted. More so than when Rebecca was alive? Maybe so, but that was only natural, wasn't it?

"Did you have fun with Noah?" He asked the question to shut out the memories of Rebecca and Becky together.

Becky considered for a moment, head tilted slightly. "Yah, I guess so." She thought some more. "Boys are a little rough."

The pronouncement, delivered in a serious tone, made him smile. "Yah, I guess they are, sometimes. But that's just how they play." In a few more months she'd be going off to first grade at the Lost Creek school. She'd have to get used to little boys, he supposed.

The mare turned into the farm lane automatically, picking up her pace a little at the sight of the barn and the thought of a bucket of oats, most likely. He drew her back a little and pointed across the field.

"Right over there, by the trees. That's where our new house is going to be."

Becky studied the site seriously, as she did everything. "Will I be able to climb those trees?" she asked at last.

He had to chuckle. "When you're big enough, I imagine you will. Your aunt Sarah was always just as good at that as her twin."

She nodded. "Maybe she can teach me."

This desire to climb trees was certainly new. Was it something Noah had said that put the thought into her mind? He guessed he'd best be prepared for lots of new ideas once she started school.

"I'm sure she'd like to," he responded. "Do you want to go and see the place where our house will be?"

"Yah. Then I can see how big the trees are."

Simon wasn't quite sure how to respond. A wave of longing for Rebecca swept through him. A little girl needed her mammi, that was certain sure.

Daad came to join them as he unharnessed the mare. His first words were for Becky. "Did you find the things you wanted for your dolly?"

How was it Daad knew what she'd wanted to find when he hadn't?

"Yah, except for her nightgown. But Lyddy said her doll has an extra one. She's going to give it to me."

Daad didn't blink an eye at the idea that Lyddy still played with dolls. "That's nice of Lyddy. And I think your grossmammi would like to make a new one for her, too."

Becky's face lit up at the idea, making him wonder why he hadn't thought of that. He seemed to be lagging behind on the whole subject.

Becky slid her hand into Daad's. "We're going to see where our new house will be. Will you come, too?"

Daad glanced at him, and Simon saw that his eyes were bright with tears at the invitation. "I will, for sure."

One step forward, two steps back. Or maybe he was the only one finding problems. Or inventing them where they didn't exist.

They'd reached the spot, and Daad found the peg, almost hidden by the grass that was springing up. "Here's where the corner of your house will be." Holding Becky's hand, he paced off. "And that means your back door will be about right here. What you do think about that?"

She eyed the trees that would shade the backyard, once they had one. "I like it," she announced. Releasing his hand, she skipped off through the wet grass toward the nearest tree.

Seeing the questioning look in Daad's eyes, he shrugged. "She wants to learn how to climb trees all of a sudden. Only thing I can figure out is that she was playing with Beth's little boy at the coffee shop, and he must have put the idea in her head."

"If it wasn't Noah, it would be something else. You can't stop kinder from stretching their wings a little bit."

"That's for sure." He repressed the instinct to say that she was just a baby. She wasn't, and he had to get used to it.

"Noah will be starting school in September, too, yah? Your mamm was talking about having Becky meet some of the other young ones her age." He chuckled. "She's been longing to have a little one around again. The twins are getting too big for her to baby."

"I'll say. I can't believe how they've grown. Maybe I can put Thomas to work when we can finally get started on the house."

Daad studied his face. "Getting impatient, ain't so? And everyone is saying it'll be a wet spring."

"Maybe everyone is wrong," he muttered. If he just saw some sign of progress, he'd feel better. That reminded him that he hadn't mentioned Aunt Bess's idea. "Aunt Bess wants me to use that storeroom of hers as a workshop. There's plenty of space, and I could get started on a few old clocks I want to refurbish and sell."

"Sounds like a fine idea." Daad greeted the plan so fervently that Simon suspected he was tired of his impatience to get the house built. "But you could do it here, if you want." He turned to gaze at the farmhouse. "Maybe—"

Simon shook his head, smiling. "You're full up, Daad. And I'd need a space where I can feel stuff out without somebody deciding to clean or somebody else borrowing my tools."

Daad might have been annoyed, but instead he chuckled. "That sounds like our house, all right. Between your mother and Anna Mae, they'll clean anything that stands still. Well, if you do work at Aunt Bess's place, you know your mamm will be happy to watch Becky."

This topic did require careful handling. "Aunt Bess said I could take her there, too. Becky has taken a liking to Lyddy."

"Couldn't find anyone better to like," Daad said promptly. "Lyddy's a fine girl. Well, you can just take Becky with you or leave her here, whichever seems best any day."

"I wish I thought Mammi would see it that way. I don't want her to feel hurt."

That was another reason he wanted to

get into his own house as soon as possible. Living in someone else's home made it hard to do want you wanted without affecting another person.

"She'll understand." Daad clapped him on the shoulder. "You'll see." He paused for a moment. "Anyway, I think so."

Simon chuckled. "Not so sure, are you?"

Daad smiled back. "It comes of having so many females in the house. I have to watch my step between your mammi, and Anna Mae, Sarah and Becky, and even the boppli is a girl. We're outnumbered."

"Yah." He moved restlessly, feeling the earth boggy under his feet. "You see why I'd like to get us into our own place, ain't so? We'll only be a stone's throw away, but it will be best."

"Yah, I know how you're feeling." Daad laid a hand on his shoulder again, just as he'd always done when he wanted one of them to listen carefully. "But there's one thing none of us can control, and that's the weather. They'll not get the heavy equipment in here to dig the foundation while it's this wet." He stamped his foot, and water squished up. Apparently satisfied he'd made his point, he added, "Maybe you'd best ask the bishop to pray about it on Sunday."

Knowing Daad was joking, he smiled. Praying to bend the weather for his own benefit wasn't something any of them were likely to do. Still, there were times when prayers for the weather were suitable, like the times Lost Creek overflowed its banks and the river flooded the lower end of town. Then Amish and Englisch had joined in prayers for relief.

But his need to have a foundation dug didn't come into that category. Maybe what he needed to pray for was patience.

Chapter Five

Lydia slipped the last pin into place in the front of the blue dress she was wearing to worship and double-checked to be sure her hair went smoothly back under her kapp. A call from the kitchen below her room had her scurrying down the stairs.

Mammi, in the kitchen, was shepherding her flock toward the family carriage. "Komm along. We can't make up time with a horse and buggy, remember?"

Mammi said that every church Sunday, so they should remember, but whether it kept her brothers on time, she'd never been sure.

"Lyddy, will you check and see if Grossmammi needs any help?" Her mother turned from putting on the black wool coat she wore on chilly Sunday mornings.

"Yah, Mammi." Grasping her own jacket, she turned toward the door to the daadi haus just as it opened.

"No need," Grossmammi said, hustling into the room while trying to push her arm into the sleeve of her coat. "I'm ready."

Lydia eased the sleeve into place and buttoned the coat, knowing that Grossmammi's arthritic fingers might have trouble this early in the morning.

"Denke, sweet girl," she murmured, patting Lydia's cheek. "Who is not here?"

"Josiah is bringing the carriage up, and here is Joanna," Mammi said. Joanna, Lyddy's eighteen-year-old sister, turned to her.

"Is the length right on this dress, do you think?" She turned around slowly. "I know Mammi thinks it's too short."

Lydia surveyed it carefully, hiding a smile. Joanna had become very fussy in the past month or so about how she looked. Since Jesse Berger had been bringing her home from singing, in fact.

"It looks fine to me. Don't you think so, Grossmammi?"

"I do, yah." She touched Joanna lightly on the shoulder. "I'm sure Jesse will think so."

"Grossmammi..." Joanna began, but Lydia gave her a gentle push toward the door.

"We know what you're going to say, but save it. It's time to load up."

Outside, the air was crisp but the sun warm, even this early. Lydia helped her grandmother in and slid onto the front side of the buggy next to Josiah.

"Who's last?" he muttered.

Lydia checked a giggle. "James, of course. Who else?" She and Josiah tried not to tease the younger ones, but sometimes they had to share a laugh.

Josiah, the oldest, was only eighteen months older than Lydia, and although he sometimes got bossy, they had always been close. It was Josiah who'd gone with her when she'd gotten that frightening note from Thomas Burkhalter.

Telling herself that was no thought for the Sabbath, she pushed it away. But she'd always be grateful to Josiah.

The past few days had been so calm and normal that she'd begun to think she'd been imagining things with Simon. He had been in and out of the shop, taking some things out to the farm and setting up others. She hadn't had occasion to go in the storeroom, and since he locked the door when he left, there had been no opportunity to get a glimpse.

Still, she had no cause for complaint. If Simon hadn't felt anything in that odd, speechless moment between them, she wouldn't bring it up. She just hoped that her own expression hadn't given anything away to Simon. Even the thought of that made her cheeks grow warm.

They reached the site of worship without too much time to spare, and judging by Daad's expression, her little brother was going to hear about that before the day was over.

The youngest Miller boys took charge of the buggy, and Lydia held Grossmammi's arm for the short walk to the barn where the service was being held. She deposited Grossmammi among the women and found her own spot at the end of the line of unmarried women, while Joanna moved to the girls who were in her rumspringa group. Beth wasn't one of the unmarried, of course, and hadn't been for some time. But she'd missed Miriam during the months the latter had been in Ohio helping out relatives. Miriam's absence had left Lydia feeling odd, stuck as she was between the rumspringa-age girls and the young married women.

Not that she was eager to become one of them, she reminded herself. She had no desire to marry. Inevitably, her thoughts replayed that conversation with Grossmammi, and her mention of Thomas Burkhalter.

That had stunned her. She'd told herself people had forgotten what happened to Thomas, but Grossmammi never forgot anything. She'd remember everything about those days, just as Lydia did.

Poor Thomas. She stared firmly at the barn door and waited for it to open. If she'd been a little older, if he hadn't been her first beau, if she'd realized sooner what was happening in his mind…

If. Grossmammi always said that thinking *if* was a waste of time and better forgotten. But sometimes thoughts couldn't just be dismissed. She could never chase away the strain of those days. She'd never forget Thomas's tears, or his wild talk. And certainly not the note she'd found. The note that said he couldn't live without her, and that by the time she read it, he'd be dead.

She shivered in the warm sun, her gaze seeking out her brother Josiah in the line of young men opposite her. Josiah had seen her face when she'd opened the note. He'd hustled her into the buggy and driven the gelding at a gallop to the Burkhalter farm, driving straight into the barn.

Thank the good Lord he hadn't stopped at the house first. As it was they were just in time—standing on the buggy, trying to hold on to Thomas while Josiah cut the rope he'd put round his neck.

Most folks said it wasn't her fault. Even the bishop had declared that she and Josiah should be thanked for arriving in time so that Thomas could get the help he needed. Thomas's own mother had told her not to blame herself. But none of it was any use. She couldn't possibly keep from blaming herself, and she never had.

The door had been opened and she hadn't even noticed, not until the line began to move. She shivered and walked more quickly, trying to bring her thoughts out of the past and back to today.

It was a relief to get inside. She moved along until she reached her usual place on the backless benches, again wishing Miriam were next to her. Miriam would distract her. But she wasn't here, and Beth was married, and Lydia felt very alone.

The remaining members of the Leit filed into the barn. At the end of the line was a visitor. Someone must have company visiting from out of town, although she hadn't heard.

She was still watching as the woman

turned around to sit. Her breath caught in her throat, and her heart pounded so loud it seemed everyone would hear it. It wasn't just any visitor. It was Judith, Thomas Burkhalter's twin sister.

Lydia was aware of the service going on around her. Somehow she was able to sing, to kneel, to respond, even though her thoughts were churning. Her prayers were a wordless plea for...what? Forgiveness? Strength? Courage?

What she wanted at heart was to be mistaken—to glance behind her at the rows of benches and see that it wasn't Judith at all. But that wouldn't happen.

Please, Lord... She reached out for help. Slowly, very slowly, her mind stopped spinning. She could think again.

It had been foolish of her to think that she'd never see any of the Burkhalter family again. They'd only moved to an Amish community in Indiana, not to Alaska. Thomas's parents had felt it best to seek treatment for Thomas away from here, and she'd been grateful—selfishly so.

Now Judith was here, probably to visit the people she'd grown up with. They were the people Lydia had grown up with, as well. Odd that no one had mentioned her visit, but people may not have known what to say.

The last time she'd seen Judith was the day after the paramedics had taken Thomas to the hospital. Judith hadn't been short of words then, and Lydia seemed to feel them again, flung at her like stones.

It's all your fault. My brother might have died, and it's all your fault. I'll never forgive you. Never!

No one else but Josiah had heard her, and Lydia knew he would never repeat the words. Nor would she, but that didn't matter. She'd heard them, and they were engraved on her heart forever.

With immense effort, she brought her

thoughts back to the service. The bishop was preaching the long sermon today, and as he often did, he was speaking about forgiveness.

Forgive as you would be forgiven. Forgive your brother seventy times seven. Forgive us our debts as we forgive our debtors.

She had long since forgiven Judith for her harsh words, but she was afraid that Judith had not forgiven her. *Never* was a very long time.

Judith didn't need to worry that her words had been wasted, because Lydia had never pardoned herself.

Poor Thomas. If she had been older... if she had been wiser...maybe she'd have known how to deal with him. But she'd been sixteen, and what sixteen-year-old was wise?

The service ended, and as soon as people started to move around, Josiah came across to her and clasped her arm. "Are you all right?" he murmured softly.

"Yah, sure." She tried to say it with a smile, but it failed miserably. She tried again. "I should speak to her..."

Josiah squeezed her arm tightly. "Don't even think about it. If she wants to talk, she'll come to you." He lowered his voice. "She should be telling you she's sorry, but I don't suppose she will."

"It's all right." She patted his arm. "She can't eat me, ain't so? I'll be fine, and you'd best start helping with the tables before you get in trouble with Daad."

"I will." He still looked worried. "Promise me you'll stay around other people, all right?"

She nodded, touched by his concern. For all his bossiness, Josiah was the best brother a girl could ever have, and the only reason she didn't say that to him was because she knew how he'd react.

Beth came over to her then, and Josiah moved off to help with the tables. The expression in Beth's soft gaze said she was aware of Judith's presence, but she didn't say anything about it. Instead she linked arms with Lydia.

"Komm and help with the serving. You know how those men are—as soon as they have the tables set up, they expect food to appear on them."

She found a genuine smile that time, knowing well how her brothers always felt about food after the three-hour worship. It couldn't arrive soon enough. Arm in arm, they headed for the kitchen, where no doubt the King family would appreciate some help.

Sure enough, Rebecca King welcomed them with a huge smile and handed each one a heavy bowl. "Denke. I'd do the running myself, but…"

She didn't finish the sentence, but she didn't have to. It wouldn't be talked about in mixed company, but every woman in the community knew that her baby would arrive soon. Very soon, Lydia thought. Rebecca's husband, Dan-

iel, had been working on the tables outside, but his gaze didn't often leave the
kitchen door, Lydia had noticed.

Such a blessing, she thought, as she
hurried to help. Daniel and Rebecca
were so happy together it hurt to watch
them, and Rebecca's son by her first
marriage would be delighted to be a big
brother.

They went back and forth, carrying
bowls and trays of food to the wooden
tables. The food was typical of after-
church lunches, with trays of meat and
cheese, bread, and the always popular
peanut butter and marshmallow crème
spread. In addition, Rebecca and perhaps her sisters-in-law had provided sal-
ads and one dessert after another. No
one would go away hungry.

Eager to avoid anyone who might
want to talk to her about Judith, as well
as Judith herself, Lydia appointed herself chief assistant to Rebecca, hanging around the kitchen until Rebecca's

sister-in-law chased her out, saying she should relax and get some dessert.

Lydia went outside, enjoying the increasing warmth of the sun. She started toward the long tables where people were still clustered, feeling oddly uncomfortable. After a moment's thought, she recognized what was troubling her. Josiah's words ran right into the bishop's sermon on forgiveness and shattered there. If she had truly forgiven Judith's hasty words, didn't that mean she should do her best to heal the breach between them?

She really would rather not think so, but Grossmammi always said that if the Lord put a duty in front of you, you had to do it. No excuses.

Sighing a little, she pushed the excuses aside and walked steadily toward where Judith, who had stepped back a little from the others, as if to distance herself. Lydia wondered if Judith felt uncomfortable to be back in Lost Creek again.

When she was a step away, she spoke. "Judith?"

Judith swung around to face her, and for a second she looked so like her twin that it was as if Thomas himself stood there.

The words she wanted didn't come, so she stretched out a hand to Judith, palm up, as if to ask for something. Judith stared at her for another second. Then her face twisted, and she struck Lydia's hand away, stalking off across the lawn.

Simon had been watching Lydia. He would have liked to put it some other way, but he couldn't. He had no idea what had just happened, but he could see Lydia standing there, her face white and frozen, pain and embarrassment written there for everyone to see.

Before Simon realized what he'd done, he'd closed the distance between them to stand between her and the rest of the group, his back an effective screen to keep others from staring and reading what he saw there. That instinct to protect had always been there when it came to the younger ones, and it seemed it still was.

Lyddy blinked and seemed to register that he was there. "Simon, I... I can't talk..."

"No." He kept his voice low, leaning toward her a little. "I don't guess you can. But if you don't want everyone here to be watching you and whispering, you'd best pretend."

She seemed to come back from whatever numbed state she'd been in. "You saw that."

"I did, but I don't think a lot of people did." That might not be entirely true, but it was what she needed to hear just now. "Just get yourself together, and then I'll make an excuse and disappear."

"I'm all right."

"You look as if someone threw a bucket of cold water over you. And maybe the bucket, too," he said bluntly.

He expected her to flare up at that, in which case he'd have felt able to walk away. But she didn't. Whatever had happened between her and that other woman had shaken her badly.

"Here comes Becky. We can take a little walk together."

Becky slipped up to him and tucked her hand in his. "Lyddy, what's wrong?"

The question from Becky seemed enough to alert her. "Nothing." She smiled warmly at his child. He saw Becky respond, but she was still troubled.

"Are you sure?" she persisted. "Why doesn't that lady like you?"

Lydia stooped down to her level, her smile becoming genuine. Becky was taking her out of her daze better than he had done.

"It's all right, Becky. She's just in a

bad mood today, I think. It'll be better tomorrow."

While Becky considered that, he squeezed his daughter's hand. "Let's take a little walk with Lyddy, okay?"

Becky brightened. She held his hand and reached out to grasp Lydia's. Giving a little hop, she skipped along between them, and much of the strain ebbed out of Lyddy's face.

Simon watched her as they walked, wondering. "Do you want to tell me about it?" He was hesitant, pretty sure he knew the answer.

Sure enough, Lydia shook her head firmly. "I'm fine. Really. Maybe we shouldn't be walking off together."

"Why not?" He raised his eyebrows, wondering what she thought would happen if they took a walk together.

"Because your aunt and my grandmother are watching us."

He glanced toward them. Sure enough, the two older women had their eyes on him and Lydia, and they were talking in low voices.

He shrugged. "So what?"

"Matchmaking," she said darkly.

He couldn't hold back a chuckle. "Come to think of it, I have seen a twinkle in Aunt Bess's eyes when she looks at us. But so what? They won't bother us, even if they chatter."

"You don't know them as well as you think, if you believe that," she said, wrinkling her nose. "Once the two of them get started, they'll drive us crazy."

"All we have to do is ignore it, and they'll stop."

She paused and looked at him, her gaze pitying. "You poor thing. You really believe that."

They looked at each other, laughing a little, and he realized he felt a connection again, just as he had when she was a troublesome little kid. As for what happened between Lydia and the Burkhalter girl, he realized he didn't even need to ask. Either Aunt Bess or Lyddy's grandmother would be bursting to tell him.

They crossed the lawn and fetched up against the paddock fence. "Relax," he said.

"Relax? You don't know what you're talking about." She shook her head, but she was laughing, too.

Simon let himself relax. They were back to where they'd startled, when she was a mischievous kid leading his siblings into trouble and he was the grownup. Or at least he'd thought he was.

Chapter Six

Sunday's sunshine had disappeared, and soon after Lydia arrived at work, the rain started. Her morning coffee guys came in, shaking rain off their jackets before settling at their usual table. When Lydia reached them with mugs in one hand and the coffeepot in the other, they were already grousing about the wet spring.

"I thought I'd get the garden in early this year. Got out my tools, bought a bag of mulch… I should have saved my time." Frank made a face. "The ground's so wet it'll take until June to dry out."

"Maybe not even then," one of his buddies said, a twinkle in his eye. "Maybe you should start building an ark."

Frank flapped his napkin at him while the others laughed. Lydia reached over his shoulder to pour the coffee.

"You just like to look on the gloomy side, that's all. Cheer up. Who wants cinnamon rolls this morning?"

It turned out they all did, not surprisingly, and Lydia was kept busy for several minutes tending to them. They kept on talking about the weather the whole time, sharing memories of famous floods and trying to top each other's stories. They made her smile, just as they always did.

Elizabeth came down a little late, but Lydia had noticed she always did after church Sundays. Apparently, the long day still tired her, but she was bright enough now.

"Are they still talking about the

weather?" She nodded her head toward the coffee group.

"Mostly reminiscing, I think. I believe they're back to the flood of '78 now. Pretty soon they'll get back to 1899." Lydia started cleaning up the counter space to be ready for the next customers. "The rain may keep people home this morning."

"Most likely it has Simon fretting," Elizabeth said. "He's that anxious to get this house started you'd think the rain was on purpose to slow him down."

Lydia's thoughts flickered to Simon. "You can't blame him. I'm sure he wants to get Becky settled well before school starts in the fall."

Elizabeth nodded, but her thoughts seemed to have moved on. "About yesterday…" She lowered her voice, even though there was no one near enough to hear. "Judith Burkhalter had no call to act like that. I was afraid you'd be upset."

Lydia tried not to let her expression change. "She and Thomas are very close, being twins. She still blames me for what happened."

"It was not your fault." Elizabeth was at her tartest. "You'd better not let me hear that you're blaming yourself, because that's just plain ferhoodled."

Turning to the baked goods cabinet, Lydia tried without success to find something that needed rearranged. Anything would do to divert Elizabeth from the subject. When she didn't respond, Elizabeth clucked disapprovingly.

"At least Simon was quick enough to see you were upset. He always has been a noticing kind of person. It was gut of him to come talk to you so folks were distracted."

"Yah, it was." She couldn't argue with any of that, but she hoped Elizabeth would stop there.

For a few seconds it seemed her wish

would be granted. But then Elizabeth's gaze settled speculatively on Lydia.

"You know, Simon needs to start thinking about getting a wife to go along with the new house. Becky certain sure needs a mammi, and he can't go on grieving forever."

"It hasn't been that long," she murmured.

Elizabeth shook her head. "Becky took a shine to you right away. Her grossmammi says she's as shy as can be with strangers, but she clung to you from the first time she saw you."

She might as well face the issue head-on. "Don't start matchmaking, Elizabeth. Simon wouldn't like it, and I don't need it."

"I wouldn't dream of interfering," Elizabeth said, and how she managed to keep a straight face, Lydia didn't know.

Before she could retort, the side door opened to admit Simon and Becky. Simon stopped to shake off his rain jacket, but Becky ran straight to Lydia, as if determined to confirm Elizabeth's opinion.

"See my new boots?" She stuck out one foot, attired in a green plastic boot.

"Very nice." Lydia turned her back on Elizabeth to help the child off with her jacket. "Sit up on this chair, and I'll pull them off. We'll set them on the rubber mat to dry off, yah?"

Becky nodded, sliding onto the chair and sticking her feet out. She was obviously admiring the green boots. "Grossmammi gave them to me."

"That was wonderful nice of her."

Becky grew thoughtful. "Mammi got me some once, but I outgrew them." Her mouth trembled, and Lydia feared she was blaming herself for outgrowing them.

"Mammi would be happy you grew enough to need new ones. Mammis are always happy when their kinder grow."

Becky considered that for a moment,

and then she gave a sharp little nod. She slid off the chair and picked up the boots. "I'll put them on the mat to dry." She marched off with them.

Lydia watched her go, and she realized something. Becky was burrowing deeper into her heart with every meeting. And what could that possibly lead to that wouldn't hurt?

The child was so sensitive about every mention or thought of her mother. Surely after all these months, she should be able to talk about her more normally. Or maybe the problem was that Simon never gave her a chance. If he didn't speak about Rebecca, how would Becky know that she could?

Her natural instinct was to plunge right into the problem—to tell Simon what she thought. She was well aware of what her friends said about her—that if she saw a problem, she'd rush in where angels feared to tread. Maybe that was true, but wasn't it better than holding back and seeing things go wrong?

Simon had gone straight into the storeroom with an armload of boxes, and Elizabeth was getting hot chocolate for Becky. Seizing the moment, Lydia slipped into the storeroom after him.

He glanced up at the sound of someone coming in, and his frown made her think twice. But it didn't deter her. "Simon..."

"Yah?" He didn't sound welcoming, but that made her more determined.

"Have you noticed how upset Becky gets whenever her mother is mentioned? I thought—"

She didn't have a chance to finish when his glare withered the rest of the sentence. "Becky is my child. I'll take care of her, and I don't need interference. Or want it."

He turned his back on her, obviously considering the matter finished. The gesture lit a spark in her.

"Really? You didn't hesitate to interfere in my life yesterday, as I recall. I don't think you have room to talk."

"That was different," he snapped, swinging back toward her with a forbidding expression.

"How?"

The single word seemed to infuriate him. "Fine. Have it your way. In future I won't interfere in your life, and you don't interfere in mine. Or my daughter's."

"You can try," she said sweetly. "But I'm right about Becky, and I was right yesterday, when I said people would talk. Your aunt Bess has already started matchmaking."

She walked out and closed the door, satisfied that she'd had the last word, but feeling helpless when it came to little Becky, who needed someone to help her.

Simon stood for a moment, staring at the closed door, baffled. What did Lydia mean? Nothing good, that was sure.

In the months since Rebecca's death, he'd figured out that virtually every woman, relative or friend, wanted to interfere with Becky. They all acted as if he was incapable of taking care of his own child. It irritated him so much that he went on the offensive each time he encountered it.

Shaking his head, he forced himself to go back to setting up his workspace. Handling the familiar tools started to settle him down gradually. He would focus on this, nothing else. If Lydia didn't like what he said, it was too bad.

But a thought slid into his mind, sneaking through the barriers he'd put up. What if Lydia had a point? Could she have picked up a problem with Becky he hadn't even considered?

He slammed the lid down on that treacherous suggestion. He was Becky's father. He knew her better than anyone. And Lydia—she meant well, but she'd known Becky only a week. She was wrong, that was all, and the sooner she admitted it and left them alone, the better.

Simon found the bracket clock he'd picked up at a yard sale shortly before they'd moved. It was a beautiful old piece with the glass front still intact. Usually that was the first thing that went of these old clocks, especially if no one treasured them. He ran his fingers along the back, feeling the temptation to start work on it now. If he did, he could lose himself entirely in the work, and he wouldn't have to think of anything else.

A knock sounded on the door, and it opened before he had a chance to say anything at all. Aunt Bess appeared, carrying a steaming mug of coffee.

"I'm not disturbing you, am I? I just thought some coffee would be a good idea. It's such a damp day."

"Denke. That does sound fine."

She set the mug down on the workbench. "Gut." She beamed. "I want you to feel at home. You can work here as long as you need to."

The irritation seeped out of him. How could he resent the intrusion when Aunt Bess was so good to him?

"If you're sure, I was thinking maybe I should put a sign up in the front window. Just so folks will know I'm here."

"That's fine. You should ask some of the Leit who have businesses to put up signs for you. They'd be glad to." She was getting excited, and her cheeks flushed with pleasure at the idea of helping him. "And we should get Lyddy to make the posters for you. She's wonderful at it."

She spun, as if to rush out and grab Lydia at this moment, and he grasped her arm. "Don't trouble Lydia. Not just yet, okay? I have to decide what to put on them and pick up some poster paper and markers."

Aunt Bess nodded, but she was eyeing him in a way that said she wasn't going to give up on whatever was in her mind. "I saw what you did yesterday. You jumped right in when Lydia needed someone. That was wonderful kind."

Embarrassed, he shrugged. "I didn't do much. I just saw she looked upset." Curiosity overtook him. "That business with Judith Burkhalter—what was it all about?"

"Didn't Lydia tell you?"

"No. Listen, if it's a secret…"

Aunt Bess dismissed that and pulled a chair over so she could sit. "Everyone in the community knows about it. I supposed you'd heard from someone."

"I didn't." Was she trying to discourage him from finding out? No, if everyone knew, she couldn't mean that.

Aunt Bess hesitated, but he realized she was trying to decide where to begin. "Lyddy was only sixteen at the time— just getting into rumspringa activities. She was such a lively, pretty girl she had all the boys gathering around her."

"I can imagine." He could. What he couldn't imagine was why she hadn't married one of them by now.

"Yah, well, Thomas Burkhalter just went head over heels for her. You wouldn't remember him, I guess. When I saw Judith yesterday, I had a feeling it wouldn't go well. Judith always blamed Lyddy."

"Blamed her for what?" Aunt Bess had a backward way of telling a story. Maybe she didn't like remembering it.

"Thomas. Her twin. Like I said, he was crazy about Lyddy, and I think she liked him well enough. He seemed as lively and happy as she was, for a time, anyway."

"Something changed?" he asked, alerted by the way she spoke.

She nodded. "Thomas got more and more possessive. He wanted Lyddy to say she'd marry him. The more she pulled away, the worse he got." She paused, studying his face. "You understand, nobody knew all this at the time. Kids that age—they don't confide in their parents much."

He thought back to his own teenage years. He guessed he hadn't, either, wanting to hold his feeling for Rebecca a secret in his heart, half-afraid to share it for fear it would vanish.

"Lyddy struggled with it, I guess. She tried to talk sense to him, but he wouldn't listen. Maybe he couldn't. He kept pushing and pushing, wanting to talk to her daad about them getting married. She got him to abandon that, but when she tried to break away from him, it seems he got…well, I'd say crazy, but that wouldn't be kind. He was sick, they said afterward."

Once again she was skipping around. "What happened when Lyddy said she didn't want to be his girlfriend?" That had to be where this was heading.

"He started telling her that if she didn't love him, he didn't want to go on living.

Said he'd kill himself before he'd let her go. Mind, he never threatened her—I'll give him that. But it was just about as bad, making her feel like she held his life in her hands."

"She should have talked to someone." But he knew even as he said it how difficult it would have been. What sixteen-year-old would want to admit that she was out of her depth?

"Yah, well, it's easy to say that but not so easy to do, I guess. Anyway she did tell someone eventually—her brother Josiah. Those two have always been close. Maybe she felt stronger having someone else knowing about it, and it was a gut thing, because Josiah found a note Thomas had left for her—a note saying that by the time she got it, he'd be dead."

"He didn't, did he?" Surely he'd have heard about it if someone in the community had killed himself.

"Not for lack of trying. The way I

heard it, Josiah and Lyddy rushed over to the Burkhalter place. Maybe they had some idea what he'd do, because Josiah drove the carriage right into the barn. They found him, already with the rope around his neck, and he jumped just when he saw them."

"Awful." Simon discovered that his hands were clenched into fists, so tight that the nails dug into his palms. "But he didn't succeed."

"No. Between them, Lyddy and Josiah got him down. Saved his life, although it seems like Judith could never give them credit for that."

Simon was silent for a long moment, thinking about the Lyddy he knew—the happy, carefree little girl, always laughing and filled with joy. It had been a harsh entrance to grown-up life for her.

"What happened to him? I take it the family doesn't live here any longer."

"Thomas went into the hospital right away. And then he had to see a doctor.

There was a special clinic out in Ohio that was recommended to his parents, and they moved out there, figuring it would be best for him. And for all of them, I suppose." Aunt Bess looked worn down by the story she'd told him, and it was clear that her love for Lyddy had deepened throughout that trouble.

He reached out to squeeze her hand. "But it's all right now. I mean, surely everybody knows Lyddy wasn't to blame."

"You'd think so, wouldn't you? Still, folks will always talk. And that scene Judith made will have them talking even more. Poor Lyddy. I thought maybe she wouldn't come in today, but she's not one to let a person down when she has a job to do."

"I hope she's not going to mind you telling me the story." He figured it would take him some time to come to terms with all of it. And in the meantime he had to be careful of what he said to Lyddy. He'd been hard on her already today, and even if he was in the right, he didn't want to add any more burdens on her.

"Ach, I'm sure she intended me to tell you. It's best that you know, since everyone else does." Aunt Bess stood up slowly and put her hand on his shoulder. "I wouldn't want you to have any bad feelings about Lyddy because of what happened. She's a wonderful girl, and the way Becky attached to her is so sweet to see. Becky needs someone like Lyddy in her life, ain't so?"

And there it was...the matchmaking Lydia had predicted. He opened his mouth to say something and closed it again. If he protested, she'd just think he was interested. And even if he ignored it...well, Aunt Bess wasn't one to give up easily when she'd set her mind on something. Maybe working here wasn't such a good idea after all—not if Aunt Bess was going to spend every day trying to throw him and Lydia together.

* * *

Lydia sorted clean silverware into the drawer, amused by Becky's intent expression as she stood next to her, watching.

"Would you like to help me?"

Becky's face lit with pleasure. "Can I?"

"For sure. Just be careful to pick each piece up by the handle, so you don't touch the part you eat with, okay?"

Nodding, Becky took a spoon, holding the handle with care.

"Gut. Now spoons go here and forks there." She demonstrated. "And we just washed our hands, so that's all right. We always put the handles toward the front of the drawer, so we can pick them up quickly."

Becky nodded again and put the spoon neatly into the proper place.

"Just right." She glanced up to see that the tableful of older men was shifting around and getting ready to leave. "Just keep going while I take care of the customers."

Lydia slid around the counter and hurried to help with raincoats and umbrellas. Usually someone left something here unless she kept an eye on them.

"Here, Frank. Don't forget your umbrella." She handed the oversize black umbrella to him, knowing his sister would scold him if he came back without it.

"No chance I'd do that." He zipped his jacket and looked out at the steady rainfall, his usually cheerful face glum. "If it keeps up like this, the creeks will be flooding before you know it."

"Ach, don't be so gloomy." She put the umbrella in his hand and patted his shoulder. "It's just a spring shower, you know."

"Yeah, Frank," one of his buddies added. "They bring spring flowers, remember?"

"Not if they drown the bulbs, they

won't," he retorted. "Well, let's get out in it."

Lydia held the door to see all of them out. Neither Frank nor his buddy Albert was as light on his feet as before, and she didn't want them tripping on the doorsill.

As usual, they'd left their tabs and cash scattered across the table, and she scooped them up. Also as usual, they'd been generous with their tips. If she had a few more customers like them, she could retire, she kidded herself.

The coffee shop was quiet after they left, and given how the rain was pelting down, she thought it would probably stay that way. Just as she finished her cleanup, Elizabeth came hustling out of the storeroom.

"Lyddy, I have a job for you. Simon needs some posters made to advertise his clock shop, so I was sure you'd do it for him."

"Of course," she said, hiding a smile

at the sight of Simon standing behind his aunt, shaking his head furiously. He thought she'd been wrong about the matchmaking, had he? Well, it was just what she'd expected, and it served him right.

"Don't bother Lyddy now," he said quickly. "I don't even have the materials to make the signs yet. And I don't want to trouble her."

Lydia gave him a sweet smile, knowing he understood exactly what she was teasing him about. "No problem. I have poster paper and markers at home, and I'll start them tonight. Just tell me what you want on them." Aware of Becky watching, she added, "Becky can help me color them tomorrow, ain't so?"

Becky nodded cheerfully. "It will be fun."

"Fine," Elizabeth said, her tone brisk. "You talk to Lyddy about what you want while Becky and I get some cookies out for a snack."

Giving Simon a slight push in Lydia's direction, she went off with Becky by her side.

Lydia picked up a pad and pencil. "So what do you want me to put on the posters?"

Simon scowled at her. "You want me to say you were right about Aunt Bess and the matchmaking, don't you? Okay, you were right."

"I thought you'd come to see it my way," she said lightly. It was no manner of use for him to get so annoyed. To Elizabeth, it seemed natural to start pairing people off. "It didn't take your aunt long to get started, did it?"

His only answer was a growled one. "You wouldn't understand."

The trouble was that she did understand, only too well. It would be better for Simon if he didn't take it so seriously, but it seemed he couldn't help it.

"Look, I do see what the problem is," she said. "You don't want people to start thinking that you're tied up with me when you have someone else in mind."

"I don't have anyone in mind." Simon sounded as if he'd reached the end of his limited patience. "I'm not going to marry again—not you, not anyone. I found love once, and I don't suppose anyone has a second chance at a love like that."

His bleak expression wrenched her heart, and she couldn't find any response.

Simon blew out a breath. "Never mind me. I just don't want Aunt Bess to start pushing you. You're bound to be upset."

Lydia suspected he was the one who was upset. She shrugged. "Not upset, exactly. It's a little aggravating, but it's kind of funny in a way."

Diverted by her reaction, he raised an eyebrow. "You've got a strange sense of humor if you think that's funny."

At least he wasn't looking pained any longer.

"You'll have to work on it. By the time she's thrown us together three or four times in an afternoon—"

"I'd rather not."

"Well, then, I don't see what you're going to do about it. I've never been able to distract your aunt when she's set on something."

He frowned, staring at the table as if he were thinking of something. "What do you suppose would happen if I hinted to Aunt Bess that I was thinking that way, but that I really needed to get to know you without scaring you off?"

"You think that would keep her from pushing?" She turned it over in her mind. "I don't know. She might be even worse. Still, I guess you could try it."

"Not just me," he said. "You'd have to at least act as if you were willing to be friends."

Somehow she had the feeling that she'd end up regretting this. But on the other hand, he could hardly discourage her from trying to help Becky, in that case.

"Just one thing. If we're supposed to be becoming friends, then you won't be angry if I take an interest in Becky, now, will you?"

Simon stiffened, but she was right, and he had to know it. Finally he nodded. "All right. But..." He seemed to grow more serious. "If this makes you uncomfortable for any reason, we stop."

She tried to chase away the little voice in her mind that said she'd get hurt if she got too close to him. "No problem," she said firmly, and slammed the door on her doubts.

Chapter Seven

The next morning it was raining again, and as Lydia drove past the area where Lost Creek ran close to the road, she frowned at the muddy, swirling waters. She didn't like the way it was rising, but she tried to shake off the apprehension. Maybe she'd been listening to Frank and his buddies too much, with their talk of flooding.

Still, the cheerful lights of town were a welcome sight on such a gloomy day. With innate wisdom, the mare headed straight for the stable, and Lydia was soon ducking through the rain, holding the plastic in place over the posters she'd worked on last night.

"Goodness," she exclaimed, shedding her wet jacket the minute she got in the door. "I feel like I've been ducked in a pond."

"Ach, you don't look that bad," Elizabeth said. She held up the coffeepot. "No one's in yet, so relax and have some coffee to warm up."

"That sounds good." She unwrapped the posters carefully, discovering that they'd come through the drive without a touch of dampness. Elizabeth, carrying a thick white mug of coffee, came to look at them.

"Very nice." She patted Lydia's cheek affectionately. "I knew you'd do a wonderful gut job. What are you going to have Becky do?"

"I thought she could color in the border I put round the lettering." She glanced out at the gray rain. "But Simon might not bring her today."

Elizabeth followed the direction of her gaze. "Maybe better that way, but I hear she still doesn't like to stay all day without him." She shook her head. "Poor little thing. It's like he's the only security she has left, and she doesn't want him out of her sight for long. What she needs is a mother."

She suspected that hint meant that Simon hadn't put his plan into action yet. "She's probably not ready for that yet, but I hope she'll let us be her friends."

Before Elizabeth could respond, the door rattled, and a second later Simon came in, holding an oversize jacket around Becky. He set her down and pulled the jacket away. "There, now. I told you it would be wet."

He sounded a little exasperated, making Lydia sure he'd tried to talk her out of coming today.

She hurried to help Becky off with the rest of her outdoor clothes. "That's not a problem, is it, Becky? We won't melt in the rain, ain't so?"

Becky considered it a moment before nodding with a slight smile.

Lydia took her hand. "Komm. I'll show you the posters I worked on. Do you want to help color them?"

She got a bigger smile in return as Becky seized her hand, and they scurried over to the table. Lydia caught a glimpse of Simon's frown and hoped she didn't have to remind him that he'd agreed to this.

Once Becky was settled and understood what she was to do, she set to work happily enough. Lydia stood looking at the child, wondering whether she'd talk if Lydia sat down with her. But at that moment the bell on the door jingled, and she hurried to welcome the first customer of the day... It was the truck driver who delivered snacks to various stores around town. He always stopped by for coffee and a doughnut when he'd finished his rounds.

"Here you are, Mike. Hope you didn't get the potato chips wet while you were delivering them."

"Not a chance," he said, grinning. He shoved his ball cap back on graying hair. "I keep the deliveries dry, even if I get wet myself. Sure is determined to keep raining."

She nodded. "A wet spring, that's certain sure."

"Nobody's getting a garden in. And the equipment out at that construction project in Fisherdale is just sitting in the mud."

With a word of sympathy, she turned to prepare the usual tables for Frank and his buddies. She noticed Becky had stopped coloring for a moment while Mike was talking and wondered what about it had interested a child.

But Frank and two of his comrades hustled through the door, and she was too busy to do anything else for the next few minutes.

When she finally had time to catch her breath, she returned to the table to find that Becky had finished two of the posters and started on a third. Simon was nowhere in sight, but the storeroom door was closed, so she supposed he was working.

"What gut coloring, Becky. Why don't we put one up on the bulletin board, and another one in the front window?"

Becky nodded, but not with the enthusiasm Lydia had expected. When they reached the bulletin board, Lydia stooped to help her push in the thumbtacks to hold the poster in place. "That looks wonderful gut. You're helping with Daadi's business, ain't so?"

But Becky seemed to be thinking of something else. She glanced toward Mike, who lingered over his coffee, probably not wanting to go back out in the wet. "That man..." she whispered.

"Did he mean nobody could go on building because of the rain?"

Lydia tried to remember what she and Mike had talked about. She was so used to chatting with customers that she could do it without thinking. "You mean about the building project and the mud? I guess it depends on what the builders are doing. If they had a roof on the project, they could work inside. But if they need to dig a foundation, I guess it's too wet."

Becky's blue eyes filled slowly with tears. Shocked, Lydia put her arms around the small figure. "What is it, sweetheart? Why are you crying?" She whispered the words in Becky's ears, not wanting to draw attention to the child.

"Daadi is going to build a new house for us to live in. It'll be our home. He said so. But if they can't work on it..."

She stroked Becky's back gently. "Just right now they can't. It doesn't mean forever. Soon the weather will change, and then they'll start on your new house."

"Home," Becky corrected softly, and Lydia's heart clenched. "Home," she murmured. "It won't be long. All right?"

Becky wiped her eyes with her fingers and nodded, looking at Lydia with trust in her face. As for Lydia, the look made her feel guilty—almost as if she were responsible for the delay.

"Let's put the other poster in the window." She tried for a cheerful smile, but it wasn't easy. Poor Becky. All she wanted was to have a home of her own again.

Ironic, Lydia told herself. She had a home, but the longing in her wasn't satisfied. She'd always felt it—that yearning for something different, something out of her normal life. She didn't know what it was. She just knew that when she found it, she would be happy.

He wasn't exactly avoiding Lyddy, Simon told himself as he set to work on the old clock. He couldn't, not if he wanted Aunt Bess to think he might be interested in her. But he also didn't want to talk to Lyddy until he'd figured out how to do so in view of what Aunt Bess had told him.

Poor Lyddy, that had been his first reaction. But what about poor Thomas? It seemed he was to be pitied, as well. He vaguely remembered the boy, as he remembered most of the young ones in the church district. Who would have guessed that boy would try to take his own life?

Surely Lydia could have found a way to turn him down that wouldn't have led to such a terrible thing. Aunt Bess seemed to think she'd been too young to cope with it, but…

He stopped, tool in hand. Was he actually presuming to judge her? Or the boy, for that matter? With a shock, he realized that Lyddy would have been only a little older than his sister, Sarah. At the thought of Sarah facing something like that, he cringed.

No, Aunt Bess was right. A young girl that age should be enjoying volleyball games and singings and giggling with her rumspringa gang. Not coping with a friend threatening to kill himself.

Should he let her know that Aunt Bess had told him or ignore the subject? He knew perfectly well what he wanted to do, and that was bury the subject so deep it would never surface again. But Lyddy—the grown-up Lyddy he knew now—probably couldn't do that ever.

A tap on the door was followed so quickly by the door opening that he didn't have a chance of calling out. He'd been so intent on Lyddy that for a moment he thought she was the one coming in, but it was Aunt Bess, closing the door behind her.

"I know you want to work and not be bothered," she said, her cheeks wrinkling in a smile. "But I'm going to bother you anyway."

He got up and gave her a quick hug with one arm. "You know I'm happy to see you anytime. And besides, this whole space belongs to you, ain't so? I can't shut you out, and I don't want to."

"Ach, I promise not to be a pest. This is your work, and I don't want folks interrupting me when I'm in the middle of making pastries. Still, I thought I'd let you know that Becky finished a couple of posters, so she and Lyddy put one in the window and one on the bulletin board. So you have to notice them when you come in and tell Becky what a gut job she did."

"You already did that, I'd guess." He smiled at her with affection. Aunt Bess delivered hugs and cookies and compliments to her many great-nieces and nephews lavishly, leaving it to their parents to provide the discipline.

"I did," she admitted, proving him

right. "But it's more important for you to notice. Seems like she treasures everything you tell her. I've seen her sitting there smiling to herself when you've spoken to her."

"Yah, I guess." He felt guilty all in a moment. "You know I've never been much of a talker. Rebecca chattered to her all the time, and I'd best remind myself she's missing it."

"What she needs is a mammi," Aunt Bess said predictably. "It's high time you thought about it, especially now that you're back in Lost Creek."

He wondered for a moment if Lyddy's grandmother was as determined as Aunt Bess was. Probably.

Well, this was his chance to do what he'd told Lyddy he's do, but he'd have to be careful, or he'd cause more harm than good.

"Maybe so," he said at last, not looking at her. "But if I were interested in someone—"

"It's Lyddy, isn't it?" She jumped on that in a second. "I knew it."

"You're not going to turn into a blabbermaul, telling everything to everyone, are you?"

"You know me better than that!" Indignation brought a flush to her face.

"Yah, I guess I do," he admitted. Aunt Bess was interested in everything, but she didn't go passing stories around. "Anyway, if I were interested in someone—" He paused to be sure she wasn't going to jump in with Lyddy's name again. "Well, I certain sure can't rush it. Not with Becky to think of. I wouldn't want her to get any ideas and then maybe be disappointed."

"She already loves Lyddy," Aunt Bess hurried to point that out.

Sighing, he started again. "Maybe she feels that way as a friend, but a new mammi is something different." His stomach twisted, and he wanted to throw away the whole thing and tell her bluntly not to interfere in his life. But he couldn't. She had loved him all his life, and he couldn't respond by shoving her away.

At least that point seemed to have made her think. She nodded. "I can see you'd have to move slowly."

"As for Lyddy," he went on, mentally apologizing for involving her, "I don't know what she feels, any more than I'm sure what I feel. And I'm certain sure this would go better if nobody said anything to her about it."

"Yah, I guess you're right. I'll keep my lips closed." She put a withered hand over his. "You know it's just that I want the best for you. I always have."

"I know." His throat tightened. He hadn't shown her how much he appreciated what she did for him, and it was time he started. "Denke."

She patted him. "That's all right. Komm soon and tell your Becky what a fine hand she has for coloring."

"I will. I'll come in just a couple of minutes," he promised, and he watched as she went out, moving a little more slowly than she'd done earlier.

A pang touched his heart. Aunt Bess was getting older. His whole family had changed in the years he'd been gone, and if he and Becky were to be happy here, he had to bridge any gap between them.

Becky worked steadily at coloring the remainder of the signs, and Lydia didn't think she'd ever seen a child that age who could stay at a task that long. At least none of her siblings had. As she remembered, they always had to be active.

"Looks as if you're almost done." She paused with the tray of cups she was holding to watch Becky put the last poster on the pile.

"I am." Becky's rare smile came again. "I liked it."

"Gut. And I know it helped Daadi, too."

Becky's reaction to that innocent com-

ment surprised her. Instead of the eagerness she expected, Becky seemed a little
hesitant, as if not sure how to react.

She toyed with the colored pens,
putting the caps on and off. "Mammi
helped Daadi a lot," she said, and her
voice dropped to a whisper. "I can't help
that much."

What was the right thing to say to
that? She'd never encountered a child
quite like Becky, and she felt at a loss.
But she had to say something.

"It's not important whether it's a lot or
a little," she ventured. "We just do the
best we can, ain't so?"

Becky's lips closed tightly. She nodded, but Lydia had the uncomfortable
feeling that she'd disappointed the child.
Murmuring a silent prayer for guidance,
Lydia patted her shoulder. "Want to help
me get some cookies out?"

At that question, Becky reverted to
being any five-year-old, and she hopped

off the chair and followed Lydia to the kitchen.

When they came back with a fresh tray of cookies, Simon stood in front of the bulletin board, admiring the poster that was placed among signs offering babysitting services, announcing a concert at the middle school and advertising a harrow for sale. He turned to smile at his daughter.

"That's a wonderful gut sign, Becky. Especially the coloring." He shot an apologetic glance toward Lydia, as if hoping she wouldn't be offended that he hadn't mentioned her lettering.

"It does draw attention, doesn't it?" She took the tray behind the counter and started arranging cookies in the display window. "I'm sure it will bring you some customers."

Becky's serious face lightened, as if she finally believed she'd helped. "I liked it. We have more." Grabbing her father's hand, she showed him the stack of posters, carefully colored, on the table.

Once Simon had exclaimed over the posters, Elizabeth collected Becky, suggesting they make some hot chocolate for a snack and leaving Lydia alone with Simon.

"Denke." Simon moved next to her, looking a bit awkward. "I didn't want to put you to so much work."

She smiled, knowing how reluctant he was to accept help from her—or anyone else, for that matter. "You didn't. Your aunt Bess volunteered me, and it's much easier to just do what she says."

His face relaxed. "Thank you, anyway." He cleared his throat. "I talked to Aunt Bess about…you know. I said that if I were interested, I'd have to take it slow because of Becky, so it was best if no one said anything. Seemed like she understood."

"It sounds very convincing." She couldn't help but be amused by how uncomfortable he found it. Was it because he persisted in thinking of her as a little girl? Or because he really had no intention of ever marrying again? She longed to ask him, but that was out-of-bounds. All she could do was wonder.

Simon nodded shortly, obviously ready to change the subject. "I talked to Aunt Bess about something else, too," he said abruptly.

"Yah?"

"Actually, she talked to me. She said… well, she explained about the situation with the Burkhalter woman at worship." His gaze scanned her face and as quickly skipped away again. "I hope you don't mind."

She'd already regretted what she'd said to him after worship. He'd wanted to help, and she hadn't exactly been appreciative. Now was her chance to set that right.

"No, I don't care if you know. Everyone else does." She found, to her surprise, that she meant it. The situation had been hurtful, but it was best that Simon wasn't left wondering. "I'd hoped Judith didn't hold a grudge against me, but…"

"She can't forgive." His voice had lowered to a bass rumble. "I'm sorry for her."

Lydia couldn't help reacting to that, and Simon nodded at her expression. "Yah, I know you were her target. But she had to be hurting a lot to act that way."

"She and Thomas are twins. They were always close."

"I guess. My brother and sister certain sure are." He frowned slightly, seeming to search for words. "I know what it is to feel as if you can't forgive. But you only hurt yourself."

She studied his face…the deep lines seemed even deeper right now, as if just talking about such a thing was hard. Was he thinking about his wife's death?

She'd heard it had been a buggy accident—had he blamed someone for it?

"You sound like you've felt that way yourself." She held her breath, hoping she wasn't intruding too much.

"If you live long enough, I guess we all do."

It wasn't an answer, but at least he wasn't angry. And maybe she was starting to understand the riddle he'd become.

Becky and Elizabeth came out of the kitchen just then, settling at a table with mugs of hot chocolate in front of them. Becky's was topped with a tower of whipped cream that looked in danger of collapse. Had Elizabeth turned her loose with the whipped cream?

Simon caught her eye, and they exchanged smiles. It wasn't any use trying to keep Elizabeth from indulging her little great-niece, she guessed.

"Becky looks better today." He sounded as if he were talking to himself. "Seems like it's a step forward and a step back sometimes."

"Maybe that's part of getting used to being here." She wanted to comfort him while at the same time she longed to express her own concern about Becky.

"Do you think so?" His gaze darted to hers. "Does she seem more at home to you?"

"Usually she does." She hesitated. "When we were working on the posters, she said something I didn't understand."

Simon's eyes darkened, and she thought it was a warning. "What?" he snapped the word in an undertone.

"I had said she was helping you by coloring the posters," she said carefully. "She said her mammi used to help you a lot. Then she said she couldn't help that much."

For an instant she thought Simon was actually going to open up to her. Then he clamped down on his emotions with an almost visible effort.

"I already told you. Don't talk to my daughter about her mother." He ground out the words. "It's not your business."

"I didn't… I mean, I didn't bring it up. I just thought—"

He wheeled away from her. "Don't. Don't think about it and don't say anything. I'll do all the talking about her mother that my daughter needs." Somehow having to keep his voice low when he'd rather shout at her seemed to make him even more angry.

That certain sure told her where she stood. He was so defensive he couldn't listen to anyone on that subject. She ought to accept it, but the stubborn determination to do what she'd set out to do wouldn't let her.

"Maybe so, if you're doing it. Are you?"

Simon sent her a glare that would have wilted someone less hardy than she was.

"Leave it, Lyddy. I can't say it any more plainly than that."

With a final glare, he marched off to his improvised shop and closed the door behind him with a sharp crack.

Chapter Eight

Lydia turned, hoping her face wasn't red. And hoping, too, that they hadn't been overheard. A glance around the room showed her that no one was looking her way. No one, that is, but Elizabeth, who caught her eye from where she was sitting with Becky. Clearly, if no one else had noticed, she had.

They couldn't talk in front of Becky, and even if they could, she wasn't sure she wanted to. Fortunately, several people came in just then, and she was busy enough to have a good reason for not chatting. They often had a small rush of folks for coffee in the afternoon, mostly Englisch. The Amish were more likely to show up for coffee and a bite of something in the morning after finishing whatever had brought them to town.

Refilling coffee cups and exchanging chatter with some members of the library committee, she noticed someone standing at the counter and hurried over.

"Sorry if I kept you waiting." She smiled at Jim Jacobs, who ran Lost Creek's water treatment plant. "What brings you in today? No problems at the water plant, I hope?"

Jim grimaced. "Don't say that, even as a joke. No, I just had a yearning for some of your shoofly pie and a coffee. To go, please."

"For sure." While she was filling a paper bag with his food, he gestured toward the bulletin board. "I saw that sign in the window when I came in. That's a new business, isn't it?"

Thinking how pleased Becky would

be, she smiled. "Yah, it is. It's just here temporarily until the shop is built. Do you remember Simon Fisher? He just recently moved back from Ohio, so he's getting his business settled here. If you have a clock to repair, you couldn't do any better, that's certain sure."

"You're a good salesperson, Lydia." He smiled, probably at her enthusiasm. "I do have an old mantel clock that belonged to my grandfather. Hasn't worked in a lot of years. You think he might do that?"

"I'm sure. He's actually rebuilding an old clock similar to that right now. Just drop yours off anytime."

"I'll do that." He collected his coffee and shoofly pie. "Thanks."

As soon as he'd left, she turned to Becky, who had lingered behind the counter with Elizabeth. "Did you hear understand what he said, Becky?" She had switched to Pennsylvania Dutch. Since Becky wasn't in school yet, she probably didn't have much mastery of Englisch. "He saw the poster you colored, and it made him decide to bring a clock in for Daadi to repair. So you really were a big help, ain't so?"

A slow smile crept over Becky's face. "For sure?"

At Lydia's nod, the smile turned into a grin. "I'll tell Daadi right now." She whirled and dashed toward the workshop.

Elizabeth was smiling as she looked after her. "Ach, it's gut to see that child happy for once, ain't so?"

"Yah, it is." Lydia's throat grew tight. It shouldn't be that unusual to see a child her age happy, should it?

Elizabeth nodded, and she suspected they were thinking the same thing. "Poor little thing," the older woman murmured. "I couldn't help but notice— did you and Simon have a tussle?"

"It was nothing, just a little disagreement." She tried to dismiss it lightly but didn't think she was convincing Elizabeth.

"Something about Becky, was it?"

Lydia tried to evade her eyes, but it was no good. And did it matter? Elizabeth was as concerned for the child as she was.

"Becky had said something about her *mammi* that troubled me." She frowned, shaking her head. "Maybe I'm wrong. But it seems as if she needs to talk about her mother."

"And Simon won't." Elizabeth provided the answer.

"You noticed," she said, relieved. It wasn't just her, then.

Elizabeth nodded. "I went out there, you know. After Rebecca died. It seemed like he was all locked up inside himself. He couldn't even talk about Rebecca. I had hoped by now it would be different."

"It's not just me, then?"

"His *mamm* is concerned, too, I know.

But what can we do?" She opened her hands in a gesture of helplessness.

"I guess, if that's how he copes with it, there isn't anything. But Becky…" Lydia gave in to the need to talk about her worry. "Simon was angry because he thought I'd talked to her about her mother. Said he'd tell Becky anything she needed to know."

"That would be fine if he did," Elizabeth said tartly. "But as far as I can see, he won't. Short of using a hammer on him, I don't guess we can make him open up."

"Better not tempt me." She was glad to know that Elizabeth felt as she did. Maybe between them, they could be of some help.

Elizabeth chuckled. "You're a gut girl, Lyddy. I guess we have to be patient with him." She hesitated. "You're not taking a dislike to him, are you?"

"No, not at all." She remembered Simon's idea for stopping matchmaking.

"I'm sorry for him, and I'm trying to understand."

She should be able to understand him, seeing that she'd known Simon well as long as she could remember. But a child's view of him wasn't much use to her now.

One thing did strike her, looking back on it. Simon had always liked to be in control, whether it was with the younger children or with his work. Maybe with Rebecca's unexpected death, he'd run into something he couldn't control, no matter how he tried.

We aren't in control. The Lord is. Turn to Him.

Grossmammi had comforted her with that thought in the aftermath of Thomas's suicide attempt. Lydia clung to it now, lifting her heart in wordless prayer.

Simon's thoughts were so tangled that it was difficult to focus on what Becky was saying, but he forced himself to respond cheerfully.

"A customer already! That's wonderful gut. Thank you for making the posters so colorful."

"I helped you, ain't so?"

His heart twisted at the expression on her little face. She wanted so much to know she was helping him.

"You were a wonderful help." He touched her cheek lightly. What was in her mind? For an instant he wondered whether Lydia had a point, but he dismissed the idea at once.

"Lyddy did most of it," Becky pointed out. "I just did the coloring. You should thank her, ain't so?"

For a moment he had no words, and his mind went blank. He had thanked Lyddy, hadn't he? He pulled himself together.

"I think I did, but I certain sure will thank her again. Let's go and do that now, and then we should be getting along home."

Standing, he put his tools back in their proper places while Becky handed him each one. Then he clasped her hand and together they walked back to the coffee shop.

A final customer was paying his bill at the counter and commenting about the weather at the same time. "Wettest spring I can remember." He pocketed his change. "And the television weather says there's a storm moving up from the south that might bring us a bunch more rain."

Lydia smiled, handing him a paper bag. "Be sure and keep those doughnuts dry until you get home, yah?"

He chuckled. "I could always eat them before I go, but my wife wouldn't like that idea." He lifted a hand in a wave as he headed out the door. "See you tomorrow."

"Another of your regulars?" As soon

as he asked the question he was aware of the edge to his voice, and he saw her eyes flash. He had to stop that. He wasn't responsible for Lyddy, and if she had admirers, it didn't matter to him.

Aunt Bess replied before he could get himself in deeper. "Yah, George is as predictable as the rest of them. Always has a coffee and every couple of days he takes something home to his wife. That's so she won't get mad at him for wasting time."

In the meantime, Lydia had seized a tray and begun clearing tables, dishes clattering. He had to speak over the noise to make her hear him, but he'd told Becky he would.

"Thanks again for those posters. That was wonderful kind of you." He glanced toward the front windows. "Once this rain stops, I'll take them around town and get them put up."

Lyddy nodded pleasantly, but she didn't say anything. He'd guess she hadn't forgiven him yet for speaking so harshly earlier. Well, she had been interfering, hadn't she?

Aunt Bess spoke quickly again, maybe thinking he needed a little help. "If George is right about that storm, we're not getting rid of the rain very quick."

"My mamm will be fretting. She wants the garden harrowed so she can do some more planting." Lydia took the loaded tray to the kitchen, coming back through the swinging door almost at once for a few more things.

"Everybody's getting tired of it," Aunt Bess said. She looked at him. "You're wanting to get started on your house, ain't so?"

He saw Becky watching him anxiously and shrugged, trying to look as if it didn't trouble him all that much. "I talked to Daniel King, and he's going to do the construction. He says as soon as the ground is dry enough, he has someone lined up to dig the foundation.

Guess we just have to put up with the delay."

Becky tugged at his hand. "That's what Lyddy said. She said it wouldn't be long, and they'd get to work so we'll have our own house soon."

He gritted his teeth. If anyone should be reassuring his daughter about their future home, it was him. But it seemed Lyddy had beaten him to it.

"We'd best get on the road," he said abruptly. "Grossmammi will be looking for us."

With a few more prolonged goodbyes, he and Becky got on their way home. A light shower continued, but it encouraged him to think maybe the weather was clearing. He got the occasional spray of water in his face, but Becky was tucked into the back and curled up comfortably.

He frowned at a spritz of water in his face. Time to get himself under control when it came to Lyddy. Just because she'd always been like a little sister to him, that didn't mean he had a right to censure her behavior now. Why had he lost his temper when she tried to talk to him about Becky? He should have explained it to her quietly. That would have been a lot more effective than snarling at her.

The truth was that he had never been very good at talking, especially about his feelings. He'd always dealt with things that way. Becky was like him, not a talker. Lyddy shouldn't feel she knew what his daughter needed more than he did.

And he shouldn't be going over and over it. Was it possible there might be something in what she said?

He rejected that suggestion promptly and turned into the lane at the farmhouse just as the rain turned into a downpour. Stopping by the kitchen door, he turned to Becky.

"Jump down quick and get into the

house so you don't get soaked." As she obeyed, Mamm appeared in the doorway and hustled her inside, closing the door quickly against the rain.

His mother must have been watching for them...and probably fretting that he hadn't gotten Becky home sooner. She'd wanted him to leave Becky with her that morning, but he'd felt uncomfortable doing so. Still, he'd have to do it sometime.

By the time he got back to the house, the whole family seemed to be collected in the kitchen, anticipating supper, he guessed. Mamm looked as if she could do with their space rather than their presence, so he stood back against the door and watched Becky helping Sarah to set the table.

"So after supper we'll have a game, yah? What will it be?" Sarah asked.

"Happy Farm," she said, naming her favorite board game, one that Sarah had taught her since she'd been here. She smiled up at his sister, and some of his tension relaxed.

Becky was starting to settle into the family. His little sister had done a good job of understanding what things Becky liked and what upset her. Sarah had done a lot of growing up in the past few years.

"How high was the creek when you came home just now?" Daad asked, interrupting his thoughts.

"Not too bad," he said, though the truth was he'd hardly noticed, being intent on his own thoughts. "Someone said the weather prediction is for a big storm headed our way, though."

"Yah, I heard that, too," Adam put in. "They were talking about it at the hardware store this morning."

Daad nodded. "We'd best not put the cows in the pasture nearest the creek tomorrow, then. No sense looking for trouble." He turned back to Simon. "Are you going to town tomorrow?"

"I'd like to spend a couple of hours at

the shop in the morning. Someone was talking about bringing in a clock for repair. But I'll come back early to give you a hand if there's any trouble."

Not that there was much they could do if the creek rose, he knew. A person couldn't contain nature, no matter how he tried.

Daad was nodding, but before he could speak, Mamm turned from the potatoes she was dishing up.

"In that case, Becky can stay here tomorrow," she said, as if daring him to argue. "There's no sense in her getting soaked."

It seemed he'd made Mamm annoyed by his failure to leave Becky with her. He should have realized that, he guessed. He had, in fact, but he hadn't wanted to admit it. One thing he hadn't reckoned on about coming home—everyone here seemed sure they had a say in how his daughter was raised.

He couldn't argue with his mother

about it, so he just nodded. But he thought again that the sooner they were in their own house, the better.

The steady drum of rain on the roof created an undertone to sleep that night. When Lydia woke, the rain still splattered against the window, but it seemed to be slacking off a bit. As she rose and dressed, her mood lifted. Perhaps it would have stopped entirely by the time she had to leave for work.

The sun rose on a sodden world, but at least it was clearing. When she took down the black waterproof jacket she'd hung on the wall to dry, only a slight dampness around the bottom reminded her of the wet drive home she'd had.

Mamm caught her arm as she started to put the jacket on. "Do you really have to go in today? I don't like the look on the weather."

"Now, Mammi." Josiah put his arm around her shoulders. "Lyddy knows enough to stop if the creek is too high. You can trust her." He dropped the slightest wink toward Lydia.

"That's right." She picked up on his words at once. "I won't do anything risky. Anyway, Elizabeth is counting on me. I can't let her down."

"You'll call us when you get there." Daad never suggested the use of the telephone, but it was a measure of his concern that he did now.

"She'll be fine," Josiah said again.

But when she reached the buggy, she found he'd put a tarp and a length of rope in the back.

"Just in case," he said, giving her a hand up. "You won't make me sorry I stood up for you, ain't so?"

She squeezed his hand, thankful for him. "I'll either come back or call to let you know I'm there. I just hope it doesn't get worse during the day."

Josiah nodded agreement and stood

back while she clicked to Dolly and headed out the lane.

The rain pelted down as the buggy turned onto the blacktop road, and Dolly shook her mane irritably.

"I know you don't like the wet. But soon you'll be nice and dry in the stable. Just a few miles."

Just a few, she repeated to herself. The ditches on either side of the road were nearly bank-full and the fields across the road were waterlogged. Still, the road was clear, and if it stayed like this, there'd be no problem getting back and forth to town.

They passed the flat area and rounded the bend where the trees pushed close to the road. No problems there, but what lay ahead?

When she came out of the wooded space to where the road lay along Lost Creek, she knew her apprehension had been correct. Lost Creek ran high and tumultuous, ever closer to the road. She pulled on the lines, slowing Dolly. She'd said she'd turn and come back if it were bad, but it was already too late. With the creek on the very edge of the road and the ditch full on the other side, there was no space to turn ahead.

For a moment she hesitated, murmuring a silent prayer. If she couldn't turn around she'd have to go on. She clicked to Dolly. The mare lay back her ears, the whites of her eyes showing, and hesitated. Lydia held her breath. Josiah would have something to say if she ended up in the creek, to say nothing of Daad.

"Just a little farther," she said. "A few more yards and we'll be past the worst. Step up, Dolly." She shook the reins.

Dolly took a tentative step and then another. It was all right…they were going to make it.

And then she saw it—a huge log surging down the creek, pushed by the raging water. Caught by the current, it struck the edge of the road and veered off, but the damage was done. Lydia slapped the lines, urging Dolly on. Too late. The blacktop began to crumble, the road fell away under the buggy, and in an instant they were in the water.

The shock of it blanked out whatever might be in Lydia's mind, and for an instant she couldn't think at all. Then, gripping the lines with one hand and the buggy rail with the other, she forced herself to think.

Thank the gut Lord they weren't out into the foaming current. She was all right and so was Dolly, as far as she could tell. But the mare was nearly up to her belly in water, and while it hadn't gotten into the buggy yet, the whole thing shook with the force of the water. They were several feet from land already, and at any moment Dolly could lose her footing.

She had to get them out. It was already too far for her to jump. *Think, Lyddy, think*. She'd heard once of someone climbing atop the buggy and waiting for help, but if she did that, they were just as likely to be swept away down the creek.

One thing was certain sure. She couldn't let Dolly drown. If the mare could get them a little closer to solid ground...

"Step up, Dolly. Come on, girl."

She couldn't see Dolly's legs, but the movement of muscles under the skin told her the mare was trying. She managed to move one step before stumbling, lurching, and nearly falling before she recovered herself. She stood there trembling, and Lydia felt herself shaking, too.

The only possible way out was to unhitch the mare and cling to her headstall. Without the weight of the buggy, they might be able to make it to shore.

Lydia moved closer to the landward side of the buggy. The water was turbulent, but not nearly as bad as on the other side. Remembering the rope Josiah had put in the buggy, she reached back to retrieve it, murmured a fervent prayer for help, and slid over the side.

The water was colder than she'd expected, taking her breath away. But her feet found a stable spot on the rocky bottom, and before she could lose her nerve, Lydia pulled herself along the side of the buggy to reach the mare.

Dolly turned her head at a touch, and if a horse's gaze could express relief, hers did. Scolding herself for being fanciful at a time like this, Lydia felt her way along the harness, looking for the first buckle. Her fingers, numb in the cold water, brushed it, but before she could grasp it, the mare stumbled in a fresh onslaught as an uprooted bush hit the buggy.

"Easy, girl." She clutched the harness, trying to shake away the water that splashed in her face. She would not let herself think of Mammi and Daad, of Josiah and the rest of the family. Nor of

Simon, who shouldn't be in her thoughts anyway. She had to move, and fast.

Clutching the buckle, she forced her fingers to obey her, struggling to stay upright against the force of the water. Finally the buckle opened. Praising the Lord, she moved forward. One more buckle, and she thought she'd be able to pull the mare free.

Fighting the current, she edged to the forward strap, her hand closing on it, but her numb fingers refused to do her bidding. She struggled, pulling at it. No breath to speak, none to cry out. In another minute—

"Lyddy!" The sound shot through her with a surge of hope. Pulling herself around, she saw Simon on the bank, his buggy behind him, nearer town. "Are you all right?"

"So far." Silly question, she managed to think.

"I don't have a rope. I'll have to come in without—"

She managed to hold up the rope she'd slung over her shoulder.

"Gut girl. Tie one end to Dolly's headstall and throw me the other. Can you do that?" He sounded perfectly calm, as if this happened every day. But that was always how Simon reacted in a crisis.

The realization that she was not alone sent a wave of energy through her. She threaded the rope through the headstall after a couple of tries before she looked back at Simon.

He'd turned his buggy so that it faced toward town, and now he came to the edge of the water, reaching out. "Throw me the rope now, Lyddy. You can do it."

Could she? Her brief spurt of energy was nearly spent. She forced herself to lift her hand with the rope. It fell short, but in an instant Simon had lunged into the water and grabbed it. Moving fast, he fastened it to his buggy.

It was going to work. He'd be able to

pull Dolly out, and she could cling to the mare and go with her.

And then she remembered that last buckle.

Her face was wet already. He wouldn't notice the tears.

"It's no good. I couldn't get the harness free. She'll never be able to get out with it dragging us down."

Almost before she saw what he was doing, Simon charged into the water. Hanging on to the rope, he made short work of the distance between them, clasping her arm as he reached her. In his hand was a knife.

Not wasting words, she guided his hand to the right strap. A few moments' work, and the strap was free.

"Hang on," he muttered. Grabbing the headstall, he forced Dolly toward land.

The mare stumbled, shook and refused to move.

Simon looked at Lydia, and she knew what he was going to say—that they'd have to leave Dolly and use the rope to save themselves. Anguished, she grabbed the loose strap and swung it at Dolly's headquarters. "Step up!"

She readied the strap for another strike, but with a convulsive movement Dolly lunged forward. Simon tugged, encouraged, urged her on, and all Lydia could do was drag herself along.

Every step seemed to take an hour, but finally she felt the road surface under her feet. Stumbling forward, she pulled herself on, falling headfirst on the road.

Dolly scrambled to safety, and Lyddy felt Simon's arms around her, half carrying, half dragging her toward his buggy. He held her so close that she could feel the pounding of his heart and hear his ragged breathing in her ears.

And then she knew the truth—so clear and simple she should have seen it before. She loved Simon. In that moment it didn't really matter that he felt nothing for her. She loved him.

Chapter Nine

Lydia struggled to gain control of herself as Simon lifted her into the buggy. Her teeth were chattering and her whole body shaking, but she was safe, thanks to Simon. Whatever else she did, she had to control her emotions. Anything else was unfair to him.

She huddled on the buggy seat, trying to force her brain to work. Were they really safe?

"Dolly…" she began.

Simon was quick to reassure her. "I'll get her. You grab the lines and move ahead. We have to get clear before any more of the road washes out."

They weren't out of danger yet, then. Simon thrust the lines in her hands. She tried to grasp them, but she was shaking so badly she didn't think she could.

Simon didn't give her time to think. He slapped the gelding's rump, clicking to him. The horse moved on, obviously eager to get away. Simon, now holding Dolly's headstall, walked beside them. After a few yards he halted.

"We should be all right here. Let me tie Dolly properly and then we'll go."

Lydia gestured back the way she'd come. "My family...the buggy..."

Simon clasped her hand firmly as if to steady her. "We can't get back. We'll have to go on to town. There's no way to save the buggy."

She wanted to protest, but he was right. A look back told her there was no way to reach the buggy, not now. She watched as Simon secured Dolly to the back. He came quickly around to the front, pausing a moment to look up at her.

"All right?"

She managed to nod. She was alive, thanks to him. She couldn't seem to find the words to say that, but he didn't seem to expect it. The rain, still streaming down, flattened his clothing against him, and his face seemed stripped down to the bones, lean and strong.

He swung up to the buggy next to her, reaching into the back to pull out a blanket. "Put that around you. We'd best get to Aunt Bess's and try to call our folks to let them know we're unharmed." He had to raise his voice to be heard over the thunder of rain on the buggy roof and the roar of the creek.

She nodded, grateful when he took the lines from her hands. Even as he clicked to the horse, they heard a crashing sound behind them and turned to see that another sizable portion of the road had collapsed. The rush of stones and broken concrete hit her buggy, and the next instant it had crumpled into itself and washed away.

A shudder went through her, and Simon drew the blanket around her, snuggling her against his side. She knew he was only doing it because she was shaking with cold, but she couldn't deny the pleasure and comfort it gave her to feel him close to her—warm and solid in the midst of terror.

"We'll not get back and forth that way very soon." He pushed the gelding into a faster trot. "There'll be a lot of damage in the valley. I'm just thankful I left Becky at home."

"She'll be safe there with your mamm." She forced her voice to be steady, thinking of how upset her family would be, as well as Simon's. "How did you come along at the right moment?"

Lydia realized she had to be feeling better if she could ask the question.

"I went in early and saw how bad it

was, so Aunt Bess called your folks. Josiah was out near the phone shanty, so she told him you shouldn't come. But you'd already left."

So of course he'd set out to find her. Simon's sense of responsibility wouldn't let him do anything else.

"They'll be worried," she said, thinking of Josiah and his insistence that she turn back if it was bad. "Josiah will be angry that I didn't turn back sooner."

She felt him turn to look at her face.

"Don't be ferhoodled. He'll be too happy that you're safe to think of that."

"You don't know Josiah," she said, making him chuckle.

As the houses of town began to appear ahead of them, Simon pointed off to the right. Lost Creek came raging down the valley, ready to pour into the river. The lower end of town was perilously near to the stream, and as they drew closer, she saw water creeping across lawns toward the houses.

"It's going to be bad, isn't it?" Without thinking about what she was doing, Lydia clasped Simon's arm, finding the strong muscles and warm skin under his sleeve reassuring.

"I'm afraid so. If it doesn't stop soon, they'll have to evacuate."

She had time to murmur a fervent prayer for those in the path of the water, and then they were in town. Simon stopped by the side door of the coffee shop. "You go in. I'll take care of the animals."

Almost before he'd finished, a figure in a bright yellow slicker emerged and grabbed the gelding's headstall. "I'll take care of them. Go get dry."

To her astonishment, Lydia saw that it was Frank Pierce. One of his coffee buddies was right behind him.

"You shouldn't—" she began.

"We're not so old as that yet," he said, helping her down. "Get inside, the both of you."

Simon hesitated, as if about to argue, but she shook her head slightly. Frank was right. This was looking like one of those times when everyone in town would have to pitch in, young or old.

Simon grasped her arm and hustled her inside, wet blanket and all.

Inside, the coffee shop was busy, but she didn't have time to notice much more before Elizabeth was wrapping her arms around her. "Ach, thank the gut Lord you're safe. Call your family right away. They'll be frantic. Then we'll find you something to change into."

While she turned her attention to Simon, Lydia hurried into the kitchen and the telephone. Most Amish businesses in the area had either cell phones or landlines. Elizabeth declared that a cell phone was too complicated for her, and she was reluctant even to use the regular phone.

Mammi answered on the first ring—she must have been camped out in the phone shanty. "You're all right?" she said immediately.

"I'm fine. Just wet. Simon had come looking for me. He got me and Dolly out, but the buggy…"

"Ach, don't worry about the buggy, not so long as you're safe." Daad must have been crammed into the shanty with Mammi. "Is Josiah with you?"

"Josiah? No. Why would he…"

"He set off to find you when we heard you hadn't made it to town. He hasn't come back."

That set up a whole new stream of worry that she knew her parents shared. "He'll come back soon." She tried to sound positive. "Or he'll show up here. But the road is washed out, so he'll not get a buggy through it."

"Yah. We'll call when he shows up. Or you call." Her daad sounded as if he were trying just as hard as she was. "You'll have to stay there."

"Yah." There was no question of that,

and her teeth were beginning to chatter again. "I have to get these wet clothes off…"

"You do that." Mammi had grabbed the phone again. "So long as you're safe, praise God."

They said goodbye without any last-minute additions, and she knew why. Neither of them wanted to talk until they knew that Josiah was safe.

Praying constantly, she took off her wet things, hanging them up to dry, and hurried into the clothes Elizabeth had laid out for her. A glance at the way the dress hung on her told her that she looked ridiculous, but that couldn't be helped now. She tied an apron as snugly around her waist as she could and rushed back downstairs.

Now that she had time to look, she realized that the coffee shop was crowded not with customers but with people trying to help. They were making coffee and pouring it into thermoses as quickly as possible, while Elizabeth directed several women who were making sandwiches just as fast.

"What do you want me to do?" She touched Elizabeth's arm, fearing she'd see strain on the elderly woman's face, but Elizabeth seemed charged with the energy provided by an emergency.

"Start heating water on the gas stove," Elizabeth said with an approving look at her. "If the electric goes off…" She stopped, looking at Lydia intently. "What's wrong?"

She couldn't hide it—she was too worried for that. "Josiah went out to look for me, but he hasn't come back yet."

"Josiah will be all right." She hadn't seen Simon come in, but there he was, like her, changed into dry clothes. "Josiah's too wily to get himself into trouble."

"Unlike me," she muttered, wishing she'd turned back before she couldn't.

Still, if she had she'd be trapped at home, and this was where people needed help.

"Don't worry," he said, and clasped her hand briefly.

Pressing her lips together, she nodded. "I'd best get busy."

She turned away, and as she did so, the back door opened. The figure that stamped in was as soaked as she had been, but he had a grin that split his face at the sight of her.

"Josiah!" She rushed to throw her arms around him. *Thank You, Lord. Thank You.*

Things started to move quickly after that. Thankful that some of his clothing was still in the storeroom, Simon found something for Josiah to wear, while Lydia called home with word that he'd arrived. Word started filtering in about flooding threatening the houses that stood with their backs to the creek on the edge of town.

Simon glanced at Josiah and saw that he was thinking the same thing he was. "They'll need some help."

Josiah grabbed his soaked rain jacket. "We'd better go."

Lyddy caught him as he followed Josiah toward the door. "Where are you two going? You're barely dry yet."

"Don't worry." He couldn't help but smile. "You look like a little girl dressing up in her mammi's clothes."

"Never mind that," she said, her cheeks flushing. "What's happening?"

"We're going to help people in those houses down on the lower end of town." He realized her gaze was following Josiah. "I'll make sure he stays safe, and you look after Aunt Bess. Okay?"

She managed a smile, but her eyes were dark with concern. "I will. You'll be careful, ain't so?"

He nodded, and then escaped before he could consider whether any of her concern was for him. Foolish, he scolded himself. She'll worry about anyone caught in the flooding.

The rain still drummed down fiercely as he hurried to catch up with Josiah, soaking into his jacket again. Josiah glanced at him, but if he was curious as to what his sister had to say, he didn't ask.

"Hope they've got sandbags down there," he said instead. "Not that I think it'll do that much good."

"Yah. Best thing we can do is probably get furniture moved up to the upper stories." He'd always wondered why those folks in the flood-prone houses didn't move, but he supposed it wasn't as easy as that. Who would want to buy them?

Anyway, it was human nature to think it wouldn't happen again. Until the next time.

They rounded the corner leading down to the lower street, and Simon caught his breath. "It's worse than I thought."

Josiah nodded. "The heaviest rain has

been upstream of all those little runs that flow into Lost Creek. If it doesn't slack off soon, it could be the worst we've ever seen."

"What we saw was bad enough." He relived those moments when he'd seen Lyddy out in the creek, battered by the water, hanging on to the mare.

"Yah." Josiah's face looked grim. "You want to tell me what happened?"

"When we get time. And you can tell me how you—"

"Look!" Josiah started to run, and he raced after him, realizing what he'd seen. An elderly man was struggling up the bank beside his house, pulling a trunk about as big as he was.

They reached him at the same time. "Here, we'll take that. Can you make it up the bank yourself?"

White hair plastered in strands across his face, the man nodded. "Couldn't leave it behind—pictures of our whole life in there. Don't leave it." He added anxiously as Josiah gave him a hand up the bank.

"We won't," Simon said quickly. He hefted one end and Josiah took the other. When they felt the weight, they exchanged looks.

"How did he get it that far?" Josiah said quietly. "He doesn't look like he could get himself out."

"Guess it's a lifetime of memories. We'd best check the house."

A police car pulled up in front of the house, and a young patrolman came scrambling to help, while an older man rushed inside. By the time they'd reached the sidewalk, he'd brought an equally elderly woman out, sheltering her under a rain poncho.

After a quick assessment of the situation, the older officer opened the back door of the patrol car. "I'll run them up to the Presbyterian Church. They're starting a shelter there. Porter, you get folks organized to move furniture and start sandbagging."

"Yessir." The young man looked gratified but a little scared.

As the police car pulled out, a town truck loaded with sandbags drew up. There was no way of driving any closer—they'd have to carry sandbags down the hill.

Other folks arrived to help—he saw Daniel King leading a group of Amish teenagers and a bunch of men coming from the lumberyard down the road. It seemed natural to team up with Josiah, and together they lugged sandbags and stacked them.

"Getting worse fast," Simon muttered as he hefted sandbags and handed them to Josiah, who piled them up along the bank. "Worse than where the road went out from under Lyddy."

"Yah." Josiah gasped a breath. "I shouldn't have let her go. I should have stopped her."

Simon grunted, lugging the bags that seemed heavier every second. "You think you could stop her?"

Josiah grinned at that. "No, probably not. My little sister has a mind of her own."

An hour passed with everyone working at top speed, but Simon grew increasingly aware that they were losing. As fast as they added sandbags, the creek took them. There was no fighting the water. You could fight a fire, but not a flood. All you could do was save what you could.

The patrol car pulled up again, siren wailing. The patrolman hailed them. "Get out." He swung his arm in a gesture. "It's no use."

"A few more…" Josiah said reaching for another sandbag, and then a rush of water hit, biting into the sandbags and nearly taking Josiah with them.

He teetered on the edge for a moment, trying to get his balance. Simon threw himself forward, grabbing his hand, and yanked him back to safety.

"Whew." Josiah pounded his shoulder. "Gut thing you're around to get the Stoltzfus family out of trouble."

"Komm," he ordered. "That cop is gesturing to us."

They stumbled up the bank to where the young patrolman was gathering men together. "School bus stuck in the run out on Fisherdale Road. We're needed."

They piled into the car as fast as they could, one on top of the other, as the cop roared out into the street, siren wailing.

"Kinder," someone murmured, and he knew they were all thinking the same thing. The Englisch school buses would be loaded with young ones trying to get home. *Stuck in the run* didn't sound good.

The few minutes it took to get there were the longest Simon had spent in months. All he could manage was a silent, incoherent plea for the Lord's help.

When they pulled up, they saw that others had made it there before them—neighbors, maybe, or passersby who'd rushed to help. Simon scrambled from the car, following the others to where the yellow school bus had skidded into the run. The water was coming up fast here, too.

They formed a line, holding on to each other. The water wasn't deep, but it was fast—too fast even for adults to keep their footing easily. Once they had enough to reach the bus, the driver handed out one child at a time. The first man passed the child to the next. Stumbling for footing in the rocky bottom, he passed the child along, and by then more neighbors were waiting with blankets.

Simon took the little girl Josiah passed to him. The child couldn't be much older than his Becky, and she was crying quietly, her little face wet with tears and rain. "No need to cry," he said quietly. "You'll soon be home and safe."

She sniffled and nodded as he handed her to the next man, turning again to Josiah for another child. The water was getting higher, making it harder to maintain his balance, but the line of helpers never faltered.

Josiah worked steadily next to him, holding on to him as the current battered them. Simon had time to realize how many people he knew there. Amish and Englisch, he had grown up with them. He thought of the elderly man risking his life to save his family pictures. He understood. A lifetime was made up of memories, and Lost Creek was where all his memories had been formed.

For a second he wondered about Aunt Bess and Lyddy, but he knew what they'd be doing. They'd be helping their neighbors, doing their duty, just as everyone else was.

Lydia discovered that there was no time to think about Simon and what had happened to her feelings—and no time to worry about Simon and Josiah, either. She was far too busy for that. The bakeshop quickly became a center for folks to share information and to stop for a quick cup of coffee before rushing off to help someone else.

Elizabeth set Lydia to making urn after urn of coffee, sending some of it in insulated jugs by volunteers to people working in the hardest-hit areas. Frank appointed himself her helper, and he brought in a small radio that he tuned to the local radio station.

In other circumstances Elizabeth might have objected, but now she didn't even seem to notice. Instead of music, the station switched to a continuous broadcast of news bulletins on the state of the flooding, fielding calls from people reporting on different areas, announcing road and bridge closings, warning people who had to evacuate, and broadcasting appeals for volunteers at the food bank and at the shelter that was rapidly being set up.

Frank, listening to a report of flood-waters going over a dam on Fishers Run, furrowed his brow. "That hasn't happened as long as I can remember. And that's a long time."

"Maybe the rain will let up soon." Lydia tried to find the most encouraging thing she could think of to say, but Frank just shook his head.

"All those streams and runs that empty into Lost Creek will still be pouring into the creek for a couple of days, even if it stops now. We're in for worse before it gets better."

As if to punctuate his words, the electricity flickered and went off. Lydia looked toward Elizabeth, noting the lines of tiredness drawing down her face. But it would do no good to tell her to rest. She'd never stop as long as she saw her duty in front of her.

"Get the water heating on the gas

range," Elizabeth said. "One of Frank's friends has been drawing water, so we should be good for a time. And we may as well get everything out of the freezer. Whatever we can't use we'll send to the shelter."

Lydia nodded and headed for the kitchen with Frank on her heels. He grabbed the kettles from her hands. "I'll fill these. Maybe you should start on the freezer."

"Denke. Get someone to help you with the kettles, though."

There were plenty of willing hands now that there was something they could do, and in a few minutes the kitchen had filled with women making sandwiches to take to the shelter and thawing cakes and cookies for use.

Lydia moved quickly back and forth, helping and supervising. The day was so dark that without electricity it was hard to see what they were doing.

"We'll soon be putting ham on the

peanut butter sandwiches if we're not careful," she declared. "I'll bring out some lights."

Elizabeth would have several lamps in her apartment upstairs, and there were a few more in the pantry. She put them out on the counter and gave Frank and his friends a crash course in operating the gas lamps.

"Just like at my grandmother's cottage when I was a little boy," Frank declared after pumping one and seeing it start. "It's a good thing you folks still have such things."

Lydia smiled. People who depended on electricity sometimes didn't know what they'd do without it. Elizabeth had electricity in the shop, because otherwise she couldn't serve food, but once the shop was closed, she went back to the customary batteries and propane. Plenty of Amish businesspeople did the same balancing act every day, treading the line between modern convenience and living separately.

Lydia turned at the sound of a clatter at the back door, hoping it might be Josiah or Simon. Instead, it was Daniel Miller, who was now married to Lydia's cousin Beth and owned a general store a little way from town.

"Daniel, what brings you here?"

Carrying an armful of boxes, Daniel was looking for a place to put them down, so she hurried to help him. The boxes were laden with groceries from canned food to coffee.

"When we heard how bad it's getting, we loaded up what we could from the store." Daniel straightened from putting a box on the floor, looking cheerful as usual despite the water dripping from him. "I have more in the wagon to take to the shelter, but I brought what I thought you could use here."

"Wonderful gut." The words hardly

expressed the gratitude she felt. "You're okay out your way?"

"Fine. The field across the road is flooded, but that won't get to us."

"What about Beth and Noah?" Noah was her cousin's five-year-old son.

He grinned. "Beth is baking up a storm. Emergencies affect her that way. Noah wanted to come with me, but I thought not this time, not knowing how bad the roads might be."

"Give them my love." To her surprise, her eyes welled with tears. "Denke."

He shook his head, maybe a little embarrassed. "I brought you a couple of jugs of water from the spring, too. I'll set them inside the back door. And I'll try to bring more tomorrow."

She was running out of words to thank him, but he didn't wait for them, just hurried out to his buggy.

A couple of teenage girls who'd shown up to help started unloading the boxes, and Elizabeth came into the kitchen to see what was going on.

"Ach, people are sehr gut."

"Yah." She turned to the two girls, realizing how quickly time was passing. "Shouldn't you two go home? Won't your mothers be worried?"

The older one, brushing shoulder-length curls back from a pert face, shook her head. "When they dismissed school early, we thought we'd look for somebody to help. They chased us away from the creek, so we came here. I called my mom, and she'll call Gina's mom. We are helping, aren't we?" She was suddenly anxious.

"You're both a wonderful blessing," Lydia said, touched, and they beamed.

The girls moved off to take cans of coffee to Frank and his helpers. Lydia exchanged smiles with Elizabeth. "A flood brings out the good in people," she said.

Elizabeth nodded, but Lydia could see

the signs of fatigue in her face and in the way her body drooped. Compassion gripped her. "Please, Elizabeth, go up and rest for a bit."

She knew the answer even before Elizabeth shook her head. "Not now. There's too much to do."

"We have plenty of helpers," she pointed out. "At least sit down here at the table and have some coffee and something to eat. It's a long time since breakfast, and you'll work better if you have some food in you."

It was the only argument that would have worked, and Elizabeth pulled out a chair and slumped down heavily. "Guess that's right."

Once she'd put coffee and a sandwich in front of Elizabeth, Lydia walked out through the front to see if everything was all right. They had set up a separate stand with free coffee and food for volunteers, and she discovered that someone had put another cup out into which a man in a wet slicker and muddy boots was stuffing bills.

"You don't need to—" she began.

He managed a smile, though his face was drawn with worry. "Cash I've got. It's a house I'm worried about now."

"I'm sorry." She couldn't find anything else to say.

"They're trying to save it. I'd better get back."

"Wait a minute." She grabbed a paper bag and stuffed baked goods into it. "Take this for the workers."

"Hey, thanks." This time his smile looked more genuine. "Thanks." He tilted his head. "Listen."

"I don't hear anything." She didn't know what he meant.

"Right. The rain is stopping." He grinned, elated. "Maybe we'll beat the water after all."

Others had realized now, and people streamed out onto the front porch. Sure enough, the sky was starting to lighten a bit, and over the ridge she could see a patch of blue.

"Not over it yet," a voice said in Lydia's ear, and she smiled at Frank.

"No, but it's encouraging, ain't so?"

He was looking at the sky, not at her, and a smile spread across his face. "You think that's encouraging? Look there."

She followed the direction he was pointing, and her breath caught. There, over the ridge, the faintest of colors began to etch themselves on the sky. A rainbow arched across the valley, getting stronger by the moment. A hush seemed to grip those who were watching, and Lydia knew they were as moved as she was.

A rainbow—God's promise that all would be right with the world. Just as it had been for Noah in the Scripture, it was a promise for them, too.

Chapter Ten

Sunlight streaming in the windows of Elizabeth's apartment woke Lydia early, making her wonder where she was. Then yesterday's events swept over her, and she swung herself out of bed. According to the clock, she'd had about three hours of sleep, but she was sure that was more than many people had on that frightening night.

The sound of coughing from Elizabeth's bedroom made her pause and listen, but the sound was not repeated. It would not be surprising if Elizabeth had a relapse after the day she'd put in. With

Simon's assistance, she'd finally been able to persuade Elizabeth to get a few hours' sleep.

Simon. For a second she relived the relief that had overwhelmed her when Simon and her brother had returned from their rescue work—grimy, soaked and exhausted, but going on some sort of adrenaline that had them talking and laughing at two in the morning.

Hurrying to dress in the clothes her cousin Beth had kindly sent in by way of Daniel on one of his trips, Lydia tried to arrange her thoughts to meet the challenges of the upcoming day. Without electricity and clean water, the town had seemed paralyzed yesterday, but folks would be bouncing back today. At least those who hadn't suffered damage would.

But the water had continued to rise, and the last she'd heard before tumbling into bed was that they couldn't expect a crest before early tomorrow morning.

That meant another full day of losses and misery.

Well, as long as they had gas and water, they'd continue feeding people. And she'd better get started. Tiptoeing down the stairs, she looked around, trying to think of what to do first. Get some coffee started on the stove, she decided, and then see if she could sweep out some of the mud that had been tracked in.

Sweeping her way to the door, she stepped out into a sunlit early morning. It was surprisingly warm for the early hour, and the combination of sunlight and warmth couldn't help lifting her spirits. Main Street looked much as usual, though there were few people out this early. She took a few steps to the corner and looked down the hill toward Lost Creek.

She gasped at the sight that met her eyes. The water had come up dramatically overnight, with several houses inundated up to the second floor. The area used last night to launch boats to take people out of the hazard zone was now under water, as well. But they'd gotten everyone out. That was the important thing.

She and Frank had trundled a wagon loaded with insulated jugs and sandwiches down the hill at some time during the night. They'd provided food and drink to anyone who needed it, rescued and rescuers alike. She'd still been there when the last couple of boats had come in, with Simon and Josiah helping bring them ashore.

"All clear," the fire chief had called when he'd finished his sweep. "We even got the dogs and cats and canaries." Like the others, he was somehow both exhausted and exhilarated.

A ragged cheer had broken out from those waiting as they hurried to help unload the last boats. Finally, when all was finished, they'd straggled back up the hill again.

Lydia stood there lost in memories until she heard a step and Simon moved next to her. He stood with her, looking down at what had once been a peaceful residential area overlooking the creek.

"Could be worse, I guess," he said at last. "We got everyone out."

She wanted to speak, to tell him how she admired his courage and dedication, the sense of responsibility that wouldn't let him quit. But if she brought up so emotional a subject, she'd fall apart, and she couldn't let herself do that. Simon was beginning to see her as a friend. She couldn't ruin it by letting him see that she longed for more.

She cleared her throat. "Did you get some sleep? And Josiah?"

Simon chuckled. "He'll be along in a minute. The guys we were working with insisted on putting us up last night, and the last I saw Josiah, he was stowing away a huge breakfast."

"Gut."

"Yah. There'll be more to do today. I heard they're hoping for help from the county or state, but I doubt they'll get trucks through today. Too many bridges down for that. Maybe tomorrow."

"So we'll get along the best we can, then," she said. "Komm. The coffee should be ready by now."

As he fell into step with her, she realized she hadn't thought to ask an important question. "Have you heard from your Mamm? How is Becky?"

He frowned. "The phone lines are down in a couple of places. I couldn't get through on a regular phone, but one of the guys had a cell phone he let me try. Mamm says they're fine. They'll try to bring water and food in today."

"But the road..."

"The road will be closed awhile yet, but Daad says he and your daad think they can clear enough on the old railroad bed to get a pony cart through, if nothing bigger."

Lydia couldn't believe how encouraging it was to think that they wouldn't be isolated from their families. "I hope Daad thinks to bring some of my clothes," she said lightly. "Everything I have on is borrowed from my cousin Beth."

He glanced at her. "Looks gut on you. Good thing Beth and Daniel are close enough to get back and forth."

As they went inside, she realized he hadn't really answered her question about Becky. Was that on purpose? She wasn't sure, and she waited until they were both supplied with coffee to press the subject.

"How is Becky doing?" She tried to keep her voice casual, not wanting to earn one of his sharp rebukes for intruding into his private affairs.

Simon frowned, staring down into his cup as if looking for an answer there. "Mamm says she keeps asking about me. Last night she couldn't go to sleep until Sarah took her into her bed. Mamm said Sarah told her stories until she fell asleep."

"Sarah is growing up to be a wonderful kind young woman," she said, hoping he'd continue talking.

"She is that," he agreed, but the worry in his face hurt her. "I wish I knew what to do. Becky…since her mammi died, she doesn't want to let me out of her sight. But I'm needed here, not out at the farm. Seems like whatever I do, I'm letting someone down."

She'd hoped he would confide in her, but now that he had, she couldn't seem to find anything to say that would help.

"I'm sorry," she murmured, struggling for words. "I think…well, maybe it's a gut thing. Becky is a smart girl. She'll understand that this is an emergency. And it sounds as if she is getting attached to Sarah and your mamm."

With what seemed a deliberate effort,

he wiped away the frown. "You forgot someone."

She blinked, not understanding him. "What…"

"Becky's getting attached to Aunt Bess, too," he said. "And you."

It didn't mean anything, she told herself. "I'm attached to her, too," she said lightly.

Treat it lightly. Don't let him guess your feelings.

It was ironic, she thought. She'd been convinced, after Thomas, that love was too dangerous to be risked. Now that she knew what it was to love, she knew true love was worth the risk. But Simon— Simon didn't think so, and he probably never would.

Simon was still nursing his coffee when Aunt Bess came down from upstairs. A quick look at her face told him two things—she was tired, and she was determined not to give in to it.

Lyddy hurried over to her, putting her arm around his aunt's waist. "What are you doing up so early? I hoped that you would sleep in today after a day like yesterday."

"Nonsense. I'm not old and done yet."

"Of course not. You're just like Frank and his friends, ain't so? Why don't you join Simon? I'll bring you a cup of tea, and you can keep him company."

Aunt Bess looked as if she'd insist on getting right to work, so he rose and pulled out a chair for her.

"Komm, sit. We were so busy yesterday we didn't have time to talk. Looked like you were feeding the multitudes."

That made her smile, and she joined him, slumping down heavily as if exhausted already this morning. Over her head, Lyddy gave him a look of thanks and hurried off to return a few minutes later with the promised tea.

"Yah, we surely did feed a lot of people, what with those who came here and the food we sent over to the shelter." Aunt Bess coughed and took a deep drink of the hot tea. That seemed to remind her of something. "Lyddy, do we have much left from the freezer? It won't keep if it's not cooked."

"Don't worry." Lyddy paused to pat her shoulder. "We got everything into the refrigerator, and I thought I'd start cooking the meat today. And I hear the church where the shelter is has gas ranges, too, so we'll use it all up."

"Gut, gut." She paused again, looking at him. "Will you try to get home today?" She studied his face. "You're worried about Becky." She made it a statement, not a question.

"I think, later. I'll see what's to be done in town, first. With the water going up until sometime tonight, they'll need help." Even as he said the words, he saw Josiah come in, probably looking for him.

Lyddy saw him, too, and rushed to offer him coffee and shoofly pie.

Simon had to laugh at his expression. "Josiah's already stuffed like a turkey, ain't so?"

Josiah grinned. "Just about. I'll come back later for the coffee. Right now we're needed. They're going to evacuate another street, just to be on the safe side."

"Right." He rose, handing the coffee mug to Lyddy. "We'll see you both later."

To his surprise, Lyddy walked to the door with them. "I don't like the way your aunt is coughing," she said, her voice low. "Did you notice?"

He nodded. "Was she all right during the night?"

"I heard her coughing a few times, but she didn't get up, at least." He could see the concern in her eyes.

"You'll try to get her to rest?" He frowned, wishing he knew how sick she'd been during the winter, and whether he ought to be getting a message to his parents.

"I'll do my best, but you know your aunt."

"Only too well." He grimaced, knowing Lyddy was right. Aunt Bess wouldn't allow herself to rest when there was work to be done. "I'll stop back later to see how she is." At least Lyddy was there with her. He was beginning to see just how responsible a woman she'd become.

He and Josiah headed down to the area where they're been working yesterday, pausing for a moment to watch the foaming, whirling water pound its way through the very place where they'd stood to carry things out.

"Bad," he muttered, knowing it was an understatement.

"Look at the size of that tree coming down," Josiah exclaimed. "And that looks like a china closet." He shook his head. "If we'd been here yesterday, we might have seen Lyddy's buggy go by."

"Don't even joke about that. I wish—"

"Now don't say you wish you could have saved it." Josiah gave him a light punch on the arm. "You saved Lyddy and the mare. Nobody could ask for better than that."

But even as he nodded, he was considering what he might have done. He didn't have much time for it, as they were quickly rounded up to carry furniture out of a house. The elderly couple who lived there stood watching.

"No point to that," the man protested, catching Simon by the sleeve. "We've been here fifty years, and the water never has reached us. Besides, if the house is going to go, I'd just as soon go with it."

Simon longed to pull his arm away and get on with the task, but he couldn't. "If it's not needed, so much the better," he said. He glanced at the man's wife, who was tugging at her husband's arm, trying to get him to leave. "I promise, we'll bring it all back. And I think your wife doesn't want you to go down the creek with the house."

"That's right," she declared, pulling him away. "Come along, you old fool. Let the boys do their work."

Simon exchanged a grin with Josiah over being called boys, knowing the scolding tone was a cover for love. He watched them being guided into a car by a volunteer. He understood. Nobody would want to risk losing a lifetime of memories.

They'd finished that house and moved on to the next when Simon heard someone calling his name. Stepping out into the street, he saw Frank waving at him and hurried to him.

"What is it? My aunt?" His heart thudded in his chest.

"Lyddy called the ambulance. She's on

her way to the hospital. I've got my car up on Main Street. I'll drive you."

Simon started up the hill at a run and then had to stop, realizing it would do no good to reach the car before Frank. Impatience surged through him. Couldn't Lyddy have found someone else to send?

They were soon on the way to the hospital, though, but Frank couldn't answer any of the questions Simon bombarded him with. He'd gone to take some things to the shelter, and when he came back, Elizabeth was in the ambulance and Lydia climbing in to accompany her. She'd just had time to shout to him to get Simon, so he had.

So Simon, hands clasped into fists, had to wait, his stomach churning. Aunt Bess was as close to him as his grandmother, maybe even closer, because his grandmother had moved to another community. But Aunt Bess was always there.

Frank swung to a stop by the emergency entrance. "They won't let me stay here, so just go straight in. They should be able to tell you where she is. And tell Lyddy not to worry about the shop. We'll take care of it."

Giving a quick nod, Simon jumped out and ran toward the door, then had to stop and identify himself to the nurse who sat behind a glass panel and controlled the door. Once he did, she pressed a buzzer and the door opened.

"The woman who came in with the patient is in the waiting room. She'll be able to tell you what the doctor is saying."

Nodding, he hurried in the direction she indicated. Sure enough, Lyddy sat in a crowded waiting room, hands folded as if she were praying. He strode across to her.

"What has happened? Tell me," he demanded.

"Shh." She frowned at his tone. "Sit down and I'll tell you."

The man next to her, covered in mud and holding his arm against his chest, obligingly slid over a chair so Simon could sit next to Lyddy.

"She got worse after you left," she said quietly. "She didn't want to lie down, but she finally got so dizzy she couldn't argue. She tried to sit down, and then she passed out for a few minutes. So I called 911, and..."

"What has the doctor said?"

"He hasn't come out yet." Her look was full of sympathy. "I'm sure it won't be much longer."

How could he just sit and wait, when Aunt Bess might be dying, for all he knew? "Why didn't you call sooner?" He growled the question, knowing it was unfair, but couldn't help himself.

"Please, Simon." She put her hand on his arm. "Just wait. It's all we can do. All anyone can do." She gestured at the other waiters in the room—people in dirty and sometimes wet clothing, some of them wearing anxious expressions while others seemed numb.

He subsided, telling himself he wasn't the only one. The man next to him gave him a nod. "They're moving pretty fast," he said, as if hoping to console him.

Simon nodded, a little ashamed. "How did you get hurt?"

He grimaced. "Tried to pull a cabinet out the door. Didn't know my dad was pushing from behind and got caught between the cabinet and the doorframe."

"Sorry," he muttered, feeling small. He'd acted as if he were the only one with problems. And he'd blamed Lyddy, when he knew quite well she'd have done everything she could.

A man walked out of the emergency area. Wearing a suit and tie, carrying a briefcase, he looked as if he were in the wrong place at the wrong time.

Everyone in the room stared at him as he walked past them and out the opposite door. Simon's neighbor gave a noise halfway between a snort and a laugh.

"Clean, ain't he?"

As if the words had released a spring, people smiled and started talking to each other. Maybe it didn't solve their problems, but it eased the tension in the room. Including Simon's. He smiled at his neighbor and turned back to Lyddy.

"Sorry," he said, touching her hand lightly. "I didn't mean—"

"I know." She smiled, but her blue eyes were still watchful. "I know."

Relief washed over Lydia when she spotted the doctor heading for them. Simon clearly wasn't very good at waiting in hospitals. Then she realized that it probably made him flash back to Rebecca's death, and she chided herself for being unfeeling.

"The doctor," she murmured to Simon, rising to meet the man.

"Ms. Stoltzfus?" he asked, fumbling

a little over the name. She suspected he wasn't from around here, or he'd have known how to pronounce it.

She nodded. "This is the patient's great-nephew, Simon Fisher."

"Ah, good. We always prefer to have a relative. Is there anyone else…?"

"My parents," Simon responded. "But they can't get into town yet. You can talk to me, and I'll tell them."

"Good, good." He led them a little away from the waiting area. "Your aunt is running a fever and coughing, and I understand from her records that she had pneumonia a few months ago. We'll be doing X-rays to have a look at her lungs, but I can't hear anything, so that's good."

Lydia nodded, familiar with the rasping sound in Elizabeth's chest during her last illness. "Will she have to stay here?"

"We'll want to keep her overnight, at least, until all the test results come back. If all is well, then she can leave." He looked harassed. "She'll need care, and I'd like to see her out of the flood zone. If the family can't do it, there are nursing homes—"

"No," Simon said quickly, before Lydia could protest. "The family will take care of her as soon as she's able to be moved. I'm sure of that."

Lydia was equally sure, but like everything else in the middle of a flood, it proved to be difficult to arrange. By the time Simon got through to his parents and they contacted the rest of the family, it was several hours later.

Eventually, it came down to Simon's parents, who took up the responsibility of Elizabeth's care. Enos and Mary Fisher, along with Simon's sister, Sarah, and Becky were all gathered around the table in the kitchen of Elizabeth's apartment. Mary Fisher had arrived with a basket full of baked goods to supplement their supplies in the shop. With a freshly baked cherry pie in the middle of the table, Lydia couldn't help but smile. Like virtually every Amish woman, Mary met emergencies with food.

"We've talked to the others," Enos was saying, "and they're all agreed that we take Elizabeth to our house, at least for the time being. Now that we've opened the old track through the woods, we can get back and forth."

Lydia had suspected that was what would happen. Elizabeth had always been especially close to Enos's family, and the farmhouse was her old home.

"Jim Foster says he'll bring her to the house once the hospital lets her go," Mary said. "She'll be more comfortable in his truck than in a buggy. About the shop—"

"Ach, you don't need to worry about the shop," Lydia said quickly. "I'll keep things going here until Elizabeth is well. And until things get back to normal, we'll just have to carry on the way we are."

"You'll need help." Mary looked concerned. "You can't handle it all alone."

"I'll help," Sarah said promptly. "I can do it." She glanced from Lydia to her mother. "Honest I can."

"I'm thinking Lyddy could handle anything she wanted to," Simon said, and he seemed to surprise himself as much as he did her. "But it would perhaps be best for Becky and me to move into this apartment for the time being. And Sarah, too, if you'll let her."

"I don't think…" Lydia spoke before she could think. All her instincts told her that having Simon here full time was far too dangerous for her peace of mind.

"Lyddy, please." Sarah reached across the table to catch her hand. "You know how much I'd love to help."

"And having Becky here will make her much more comfortable," Simon added. "She'd just be in the way when you're nursing Aunt Bess, Mamm, and I don't like her to deal with any more upheaval.

Not that you wouldn't take wonderful gut care of her," he added hastily.

Simon was concentrating on swaying his parents to his way of thinking, Lydia told herself. He wasn't thinking of her at all. Of course he wasn't. He had no idea she'd been so foolish as to fall in love with him.

Mary nodded reluctantly. "I suppose so. But it's really up to Lyddy, isn't it?"

"For sure," Simon said, turning his gaze on her. "Please, Lyddy?" he said, repeating his sister's words with a slight smile.

Her heart seemed to tremble at that smile, and she knew she didn't have a choice. No matter what it did to her, she had to agree.

"Yah," she said. "That will be fine."

Chapter Eleven

When Lydia got home that night, driving Dolly along the railroad bed with the pony cart Daad had brought in for her, she decided she could handle the challenging days as long as she could get home and sleep in her own bed at night. In fact, when she reached her bedroom to clean up for supper, the bed was so appealing it was all she could do not to slip under her quilt and escape into sleep.

Selfish, she chided herself. There were still people in town who wouldn't be able to sleep in their own beds for a number of nights to come. So she splashed some cold water on her face and hurried downstairs to help get supper on.

Once the whole family was gathered around the table, Daad bowed his head in the sign to begin their silent prayer. It struck her that Daad held the silence longer, and she knew why. They were all praying for whatever would come when Lost Creek crested sometime in the night.

Food started to circulate around the table. Josiah, heaping a mound of mashed potatoes on his plate, glanced at Daad. "Did you hear that the highway department is talking about running a new road alongside the old one, but farther from the creek?"

"I heard." Daad grimaced. "Whatever they do, it'll take time. We'll have to get used to using the railroad bed until then. Lyddy, how was it when you drove home?"

Her mind was several miles away, but

she managed to collect herself. "Not bad. It was boggy in one spot, but Dolly got through. She gave me a look about being hitched to the pony cart, though."

Josiah laughed. "She's spoiled, that's what. If she'd gotten the buggy out of the creek—"

"Don't," Mammi said sharply. "That is nothing to joke about. Just thank the gut Lord for preserving our Lyddy. And Dolly."

"Yah, I do." Josiah looked abashed, and Lyddy gave him an understanding look. They'd both seen so much sorrow in the past days that it was better to joke than to weep.

"I know the spot you mean," Daad said, firmly changing the subject. "If I can get a load of gravel, we'll be able to make that better. We can take it up in the old spring wagon."

Josiah nodded. "I'll help. We could do it in no time. It'd be gut to have it done before they try to bring Elizabeth out to the Fishers' place."

"So Simon and Becky will be moving into Elizabeth's apartment, I hear." Grossmammi's gaze grew thoughtful, and Lydia hoped that wasn't matchmaking she had in her eyes. "I'm not sure how much help he'll be in the coffee shop, but it's better than having the place empty. Or you being there alone, Lyddy."

"I'm sure he'll find something to do." She was determined to put a good face on the situation. "Elizabeth wants me to keep on offering free coffee and drinks to all the volunteers, and another pair of hands will help. And his sister is coming in, as well. She'll watch Becky along with helping in the kitchen."

"I'll bake tomorrow," Mammi said, eyes glowing at the thought of cooking for more people. "And Dorie said to tell you she'll be bringing some things to the bake shop, as well."

Dorie, Lydia's older sister, lived with her family on the other side of town, so she shouldn't have trouble coming in. She just hoped Dorie wouldn't bring her three-year-old twins along. Much as Lydia loved her little nephews, she hated the thought of having those two active boys run free through the coffee shop.

"That will be a big help," she said, her words interrupted by an enormous yawn.

"Ach, you've had such a couple of days." Mammi began gathering up plates. "After dessert you'll go straight to bed."

She hated to admit how wonderful that sounded. "I'll help with the dishes—" she began, but Mammi interrupted her.

"You'll do no such thing. As if I can't manage them by myself. Sleep is the best thing for you right now."

Josiah grinned. "You might as well give in. I'd guess no one will tell me or

Simon to go to bed early, and we put in a long day, too."

"You go up early, as well," Mammi scolded. "And I'd tell Simon the same if I had him under my wing."

Lydia began serving the cherry pie Mammi had cut, and she managed to elbow her brother while she did it. "You mind Mammi too, you hear?"

He gave her a mock glare. "I'll say this, I found out hauling furniture isn't so easy, especially on stairs. And when folks are following you around, all upset, it's even worse."

Mamm clucked in sympathy, looking as if she'd take all those folks in, if she could. Of course she would. Everyone would do what they could in a crisis like this. But it would still be a long road back for some of those people.

Half an hour later, Lydia was twisting her hair into a long, loose braid, ready to slip into bed, when someone rapped softly.

"Komm." Maybe Mammi, wanting to fuss a little more.

But it was Grossmammi. "Let's talk a few minutes before you sleep," she said, closing the door.

Lydia sat down and patted the bed beside her. "I can always stay awake for you."

"Ach, that's ferhoodled, for sure." Grossmammi settled herself and clasped her hand. "Now tell me the things you didn't say. About Simon."

Lydia could only stare at her for a long moment. Denying it would be useless. Grossmammi would always know the truth. "I love him," she whispered. "I never thought, after what happened with Thomas, that I could love someone."

"That was even more ferhoodled," Grossmammi said. "What happened to Thomas was not your fault, and he's alive to make a new start because of you and Josiah. It has nothing to do with what you feel for Simon."

"No. It doesn't." And she was able to believe that was true. "But Simon doesn't think of me that way. Even if he did," she hesitated, "I know he hasn't accepted losing Rebecca."

"Let me tell you a secret," Grossmammi said. "Most times men don't notice what's right in front of them until they're pushed into it."

She couldn't help smiling at her grandmother's philosophy. "I don't think I'd be very good at pushing him. And Rebecca..." Her throat tightened at the thought of his loss and Becky's.

Grossmammi's fingers tightened on hers. "Are you sure? It's been nearly a year, and he did come back."

Her eyes filled with tears. "He won't talk about her. Can't talk about her, even to Becky. And that child needs to know what to think about her mammi. She's all tied up inside with it."

"Have you talked to her?"

That was a sore spot. "I would, but

any mention of her mother to Becky makes Simon so angry. He says he'll tell her anything she needs to know. But he doesn't."

"Sounds like he needs something to force him into it." Grossmammi gave a short nod. "I'll pray on it."

Lydia blinked away tears. "Denke," she murmured, although she couldn't imagine what that something would be. She was silent for a moment, trying to recover herself. "But even so, I don't think he'll ever love someone else the way he loved Rebecca."

Her grandmother studied her face for a long moment, her eyes filled with the wisdom of years. "Maybe not," she said finally. "She was his first love. But that doesn't mean she has to be his only love. There is always room in the heart for more."

Lydia wanted, so much, to believe that. But she didn't know if she could.

* * *

Lydia had just finished making the first pot of coffee at the shop the next morning when she heard noises at the kitchen door. She turned to greet Becky, who came running to give her such a big hug it seemed she hadn't seen Lydia for a week.

"Lyddy, I'm back," she said, and the happiness in her face melted Lydia's heart. How could she object to having Simon and Becky living here when it obviously meant so much to the child?

"I'm wonderful glad to see you." She glanced over Becky's head to smile at Simon and Sarah.

Simon just nodded in greeting, but Sarah looked almost as happy as Becky. Tying an apron around her waist, she hurried to Lydia. "I'm ready to help. Just tell me what I should do."

Deciding to take her at her word, Lydia sent her off to the storeroom to bring in a fresh supply of paper cups. The coffee shop normally served its coffee in the thick white mugs most people preferred, but until they had water coming out the spigot, it would be impossible to keep enough of them washed.

"What can I do?" Becky tugged at her hand, but Simon grasped the child's shoulder for a moment.

"Just let me have a word with Lyddy, and then you can talk," he said.

Becky nodded, agreeable as always to anything her father suggested. It occurred to Lydia that she'd never even seen Becky pout a little at an unpopular suggestion. Lyddy appreciated cooperative children, but somehow a little dissatisfaction would seem more normal.

But Simon was claiming her attention. "I'll bring in the jugs of spring water I brought with me, and then I think I'd best see what happened when the water crested. I'll probably be needed there again today."

"We'll be fine here. Won't we, Becky?"

She got the expected nod. "Come back and tell us about it when you have time. And tell any of the volunteers you see that there's free coffee and snacks again today."

He nodded and bent to give Becky a hug. "Don't forget to help and be sure to tell Sarah or Lyddy if you need anything."

Without waiting for a response, he turned and was gone in a few long strides.

She would not stand here staring after him. There was work to be done.

Sarah returned with the cups, and together they began to get the shop ready to open. Becky trailed behind them, helping everywhere she could, and Lyddy soon realized she'd have to find something to occupy the child, especially when they were carrying pots of hot water around the kitchen.

Luckily she had just the project at hand. "Becky, we need to put up a couple of new signs, so that people who are helping in the flood area know they can have free coffee. Do you want to help with those?"

That was a project after Becky's heart, as she knew, and in a few minutes the little girl was settled at a small table ready to color in and decorate the wording Lydia had done.

Sarah smiled when Lydia returned to the kitchen. "Becky sure loves to color and draw. That will keep her busy."

"And doing something helpful." She glanced back in Becky's direction, loving the total concentration on her face. "That seems really important to her... that she's helping, especially her daadi."

"Yah, I noticed that, too." Sarah bent over the oven, pulling out the pan of cinnamon rolls she'd been warming. She hadn't waited to be asked. She'd just done it. Clearly, she was another person who wanted to be helpful.

With her dark brown hair and eyes,

Sarah looked very much like her older brother. Fortunately, Lydia thought, she didn't have his square, stubborn jaw.

"I'll open the door. We're as ready as we can be."

When she reached the door, she found that Frank and his buddies had already arrived. "Come in. You're early today."

"We've all got jobs for the day," he said, obviously relishing having something important to do. "Some at the shelter and some at the food bank. But we have to have our coffee, first."

"Coming right up," she said. "You know it's free to you in return for all your volunteering."

She could hear them teasing each other about who deserved free coffee, and then the shop started to get busy. She didn't get back to their table until they were leaving and wasn't surprised at all to find that someone had left money on the table, despite her offer. But that was the sort of people they were, she knew.

She put the money in the box they were using for a cash register until the electricity came back on.

The morning seemed to fly past, almost as fast as the rumors that were flying about what was going to happen when. Apparently, assistance hadn't arrived from the state yet, but the Salvation Army was already busy finding housing for those who were displaced.

"It must be awful not to even know what you can save from your house," Sarah commented, loading a tray. "I feel so bad for them."

"I'm sure your brother will have some stories to tell about it when he gets back. At least folks are doing everything possible to help them." She paused for a moment while Sarah carried the tray of doughnuts to the front, thinking how useful the girl was being.

"What next?" Sarah said, coming back.

"Next I think you should sit down and have something to eat for yourself." Lydia gestured toward the table. "I'll take care of the front, but it looks as if we'll have a lull for a bit."

"I'm fine," Sarah protested. "This is the most fun I've had in a long time."

It occurred to Lydia that the girl was probably doing the very things that she'd consider chores at home. But being here was different, and that was important at Sarah's age.

"You like getting out of the house, I guess," she ventured.

"For sure." Sarah poured a cup of coffee for each of them. "Did you know that my twin is going to start as an apprentice at the machine shop this summer? He's not a bit older than me, but when I told Mammi I wanted a job like him, she wouldn't listen."

"Working in a machine shop?" Lydia asked, smiling.

Sarah giggled. "That would be fun, wouldn't it? But I'd like to work in a restaurant or here, in the coffee shop.

I don't see why I shouldn't learn to do something useful."

Lydia couldn't agree more, but she decided it wouldn't be right to say so. Not unless she wanted to get into trouble with Sarah's parents.

"Everyone has a job but me," Sarah said, a trace of rebellion in her voice.

"You know, when Simon sees how capable you are here, he might be willing to talk to your parents about it," she suggested. Simon wouldn't appreciate her interference, she guessed, but Sarah deserved some encouragement.

"You feel he might?" Her face lit up at the thought.

"It's worth a try," she said. "Since we're not so busy right now, I'm going to run upstairs and see what needs to be done for tonight."

"All right," Sarah called after her. "But I'll do it."

Smiling, she went lightly up the stairs. Sarah was really mature for her fourteen years. Maybe, like everyone else, she was rising to the occasion.

One of the bedroom doors stood open, so she headed for it first, making a mental note that the beds would have to be changed. When Lydia stepped inside, everything she was thinking flew out of her head.

Becky sat on the edge of the bed. She had taken her braid down from under her kapp, and as Lydia watched, she picked up a red marker and started to color a strand of corn silk blond hair.

"Becky, stop." She hurried over to the child, reminding herself that she must be careful. Simon wouldn't want her to interfere, but he also wouldn't want his daughter to color her hair red.

Becky looked up at the sound of her voice, clutching the marker, and her face set stubbornly. "I want to color my hair."

Gently, she reminded herself. "You do? I don't think markers are very good for that." She took the marker from the child's hand, relieved that Becky didn't resist.

"I want to," she repeated.

"I see that you do." There was something almost desperate in the set look of the child's face, and she prayed silently for guidance, her heart aching. "But why? I think you have pretty hair."

For a moment she thought Becky wouldn't answer, and she wished Simon was here to deal with his daughter. But then Becky looked up at her, blue eyes filling with tears.

"People keep saying I'm like my mammi. But I'm not. I'm not! Mammi could do everything. I can't do anything."

Dropping the marker, Lydia gathered Becky's hands in hers. Her throat was so tight she struggled to speak, and she had to. She had to assure this precious child that she was unique and loved.

"Becky, you have it all wrong. Really. Mammi was a grown-up woman, and you're such a little girl. I think by the time you grow up, you'll be able to do all the things Mammi did, and maybe even more."

Becky's expression didn't change. She was failing to get through to her.

"People say it. All the time."

"People say silly things sometimes." Herself included. But who could guess the child would interpret the innocent words that way? "They're just trying to start talking to you. They mean that you look like your Mammi did when she was a little girl. That's all."

Some of the tension drained from her face. "Are you sure?"

"Yah. I'm positive. I said it to you, and that's what I meant."

Becky considered the words, her face serious. "But…if I'm not like Mammi, will Daadi love me just as much?"

"Ach, Becky, of course he will." Her grandmother's words slipped into her mind, and she clung to them. "There's always room in the heart for more love."

Hope dawned slowly on Becky's face. Then she threw herself into Lydia's arms. Tears spilling over, Lydia held her close. A faint sound made her glance toward the door. Simon stood there. Watching. Listening. And she couldn't tell what he was thinking.

Simon froze, immobile with shock from the power of that conversation. He shook it off, trying to be angry with Lyddy for talking to Becky about her mother after he'd made his feelings clear. But he couldn't. He couldn't, because however it had happened, Becky had turned to Lyddy, not to him. Lyddy had brought out the things that he needed to know about his daughter.

This wasn't a time for recriminations. Lyddy had already seen him, and in a moment, Becky might turn and spot him, too. Praying for the right words to say, he walked quietly into the room.

Lyddy moved, as if she'd get up and leave the room, but he gestured her to stay. She was in this now, like it or not. Becky looked up, saw him and huddled against Lyddy, the gesture hurting his heart.

"Lyddy is right, ain't so?" He sat down next to them, touching his daughter gently. "There's always room for love in your heart. Your mammi taught me that, and I know she wants you to know it, too."

Becky looked up at him, blue eyes wide and wondering. "You...you're sure?"

"I'm sure."

"You see?" Lyddy said. "You don't need to color your hair or try to be perfect. Daadi loves you just the way you are."

He spotted the markers scattered on the quilt as Lyddy touched Becky's braid lightly. Why would she think…? But that didn't matter right now. What mattered was that his daughter know he loved her more than anything.

Stroking her hair, he smiled at her, hoping she couldn't see the tears in his eyes. "I would love you just the same if your hair was purple with green stripes. Okay?"

Becky giggled, and the tension seemed to vanish as if it had never been. "Mammi wouldn't like purple and green, would she?"

"Probably not. You know, when you were a tiny baby, you had a little wisp of blond hair right on top of your head. And Mammi said it was the prettiest curls she'd ever seen."

"She did?"

But even as he nodded, her little face clouded up again.

"Sometimes…sometimes I can't remember things about Mammi," she whispered. "I don't want to forget."

Simon felt as if he'd been stabbed in the heart. How could he have been so thoughtless? How could he have understood so little?

"You know, I think that's because we haven't talked enough about her." And it was his fault. "Suppose we make an agreement between us. Whenever you want to talk about Mammi, I'll help you remember. And you'll do the same for me. All right?"

Her smile blossomed. To his surprise, his daughter reached out and patted his cheek as if to comfort him. "I promise, Daadi."

His throat closed completely, and he couldn't possibly speak. He looked at Lyddy in a wordless appeal for help.

"I think we'd better go back and help Sarah, don't you think? She probably needs us."

"Okay." Becky hopped off the bed as if none of this had happened. "I'll help."

As Lydia moved to follow her, Simon touched her arm. "Denke, Lyddy. Denke."

He should say more, but he couldn't. He'd have to hope she understood. But as they walked down the steps together, he realized he didn't need to worry about that. Lyddy was probably the most understanding person he knew.

Chapter Twelve

By the next morning, Lydia had come to terms with her feelings. As she drove up the trail to the woods and then turned onto the makeshift road, the sunlight filtering through the trees seemed a promise of better things to come. If not for her, then at least for Simon and his daughter. She had to rejoice over that, and she did.

She had feared, in those first moments after she'd seen Simon standing at the door listening to his daughter, that his reaction would be an explosion of wrath against her. But Simon had finally listened instead of closing his heart, and the results could only be good. He'd opened up to his daughter at last, and Becky's response was lovely. Her heart warmed again at the memory of that small child patting her father's cheek to comfort him.

If only she could comfort him, but she knew she couldn't. Not unless he opened up to her the way he had to his daughter, and she'd seen no signs that he'd even thought of doing that.

Lost Creek looked better this morning, she decided. Not back to normal yet, but with the sun shining and the streets dry again, the few people she saw looked more cheerful than they had for the past two days.

Stabling Dolly, she hurried inside, to be met by the fragrance of brewing coffee. Clearly, Sarah had remembered what Lydia had told her. With all their dependence now on the gas stove, it was a juggling act to get everything done.

Sarah turned from the stove at the sound of her footsteps and gave her a beaming smile. "The coffee is ready. Can I pour a cup for you?"

Instinct told her the girl would be disappointed if she refused. "Smells wonderful gut. Yah, I'd love one. It was still a little chilly when I left home."

Hanging up her heavy sweater, she scrubbed her hands and did a quick check of the kitchen. Sarah had gone above and beyond, with a pan of breakfast cake just coming out of the oven, and several trays of rolls ready to go out front.

"Everything looks fine." She checked the clock. "We'll open in fifteen minutes, so if you haven't eaten, now's the time."

Sarah giggled. "My bruder fixed breakfast for us this morning. I never knew that Simon could cook eggs. Or anything else." She poured coffee for both of them and brought the cups to the table. "I wish we could use the regular mugs. I think the paper cups give a different taste."

"Don't say that to any of the customers." The voice came from above them as Simon came down the steps, with Becky skipping alongside him. Becky darted ahead of her father to give Lydia a hug.

Lydia hugged her back, marveling at the change a few hours had made in Becky. Now she looked like a normal, happy little girl instead of the anxious, fearful little mouse she'd been.

"Have you had breakfast already?" she asked.

Becky nodded vehemently. "My daadi made breakfast. He makes wonderful gut dippy eggs." She smiled up at Lydia. "He'll make some for you, ain't so, Daadi?"

If that had caused Simon any embarrassment, she'd have found it encouraging, but he just smiled and turned to check the front of the shop.

She was thankful to God for what had happened between Simon and Becky, she told herself fiercely. She didn't expect anything else. But her unruly heart denied the words even as she thought them. All this time that she'd been uninterested in marriage—now she knew it hadn't been just wariness. It had been because she was waiting for Simon. But she couldn't say the same about him.

"Time to open," she said cheerfully. "Do you think we're ready, Sarah?"

Pleased at being consulted, Sarah nodded, then was attacked by a sense of caution. "I think. If I missed anything, you'll tell me, won't you?"

Lydia smiled, nodding. Sarah had learned a great deal in just a day. "I promise. Let's do it."

In a few minutes they were busy with the usual morning rush. Lydia threw herself into work, relieved for the distraction from her own thoughts.

As the rush was abating, Frank and his friends came in, and she hurried to get their table ready. Responding to their usual greetings and joking felt like getting back to normal for about a minute. Then they started updating her on all the news, and Simon came over to listen.

"The crest came through about one a.m., near as I could tell," Frank said. "The rumor is there's considerable damage to the water treatment plant, so no water in the pipes for a week or more."

"You should hear my wife on the subject," somebody else complained. "She'll have me hauling water all day if she has her way."

"So that's why you're here." Frank grinned at him. "Anyway, they're going to let people on Tenth Street back into their houses today. Water didn't reach the first floor, thank goodness."

Simon noticeably relaxed, and she remembered he'd been moving furniture from those houses the previous day. "They'll have a lot to do," he pointed out.

Frank nodded. "They're asking for help, but not before ten o'clock. Guess the emergency management people have to okay it first."

Simon glanced at the clock. "I'll go down then if you can spare me here." He looked at Lydia as if she were in charge.

"Whatever you want," she said. "We'll manage."

Frank started talking about their plans to run food and beverages down to the workers later, and by the time she looked up again, Simon was gone.

Forcing herself to focus on what they could supply, she went back to the kitchen. She and Sarah were quickly immersed in work, with Becky running back and forth being helpful.

It was nearly ten when Simon reappeared in the kitchen. "Can you come out for a minute, Lyddy?" he asked. "I want to show you where I'm putting the water jugs that Daniel King brought in."

With a quick glance to be sure everything was running properly, Lydia followed him.

Simon led her to the shed attached to the stable, but once there, he seemed to forget why they'd come.

"The water storage?" she reminded him, sensing tension and not knowing how to account for it.

"Ach, I didn't need to haul you out here just for that." He gestured at a row of water jugs. "You can see for yourself. I just…" He seemed to run out of words.

Lydia studied his face, trying not to think about how dear it had become to her. "Is something wrong?"

"No, no." Prompted, he seemed to find he could go on. "I hardly had a chance to thank you yesterday. And you have to know how much I appreciate what you did. Even when I told you not to." He gave her a rueful grin.

"That's all right. I was butting in and trying to take charge, like always. My cousin Miriam says I'm like a tornado sweeping up everything in my path once I get started."

It would be easier for both of them to turn it off lightly than to talk about it seriously.

But from the way Simon was shaking his head, it seemed he wouldn't let her get away with that. "When I put Becky to bed last night, we sat for a long time talking about her mammi." He grimaced. "I'm her father. I should have seen how much she needed to talk. You did."

"Ach, don't think that." She could hardly get the words out fast enough. "You were trying to handle your own grief." She saw his face tighten at that and slipped away from such dangerous territory. "It's often easier for an outsider to see a problem than the person who's involved."

That made it sound as if she weren't involved. She was, with her whole heart, but she couldn't say that to him.

"Even so…"

She understood his reluctance to let go of the blame, and she wasn't sure anyone could help him with that. But she had to try.

"You couldn't help it, Simon. Nobody could. I know you feel responsible…"

"I am responsible." His voice was filled with passion. "I was responsible for taking care of Rebecca, and I failed her. And then I failed her daughter."

Somehow she knew soft words wouldn't help now. "Don't be so ferhoodled," she said sharply. "You couldn't have predicted the accident. Or prevented it."

"If I'd been driving the buggy—"

"If you had been driving the buggy, maybe you'd both be gone, and Becky would be left alone. How would that help anyone?" Afraid to say too much and afraid to say too little, she stopped.

"I know what I know." His stubbornness had never been more pronounced. He pushed the door open and held it for her. "I'll always be thankful you helped Becky, Lydia. But don't try to help me. No one can do that."

Obeying his gesture, she walked out of the shed. He was right. As long as he felt the way he did, no one could help him.

Simon walked down the slight hill toward the creek, but his thoughts were still on Lyddy. It was as natural as breathing for her to want to help, but in this case she couldn't, and it was best she realized it.

He didn't want to hurt her. That was uppermost in his mind at the moment. It had become crucial that Lyddy not be hurt, by him or by anyone else.

He reminded himself that he had no

responsibility to Lyddy except as a friend, but that didn't seem to make a difference to his feelings. He'd known her since childhood, and he owed her a debt he could never repay.

Forcing himself away from thoughts of Lydia, he tried to focus on the scene in front of him. The creek was fast, roiled and muddy, but it had gone down visibly, leaving behind it a sea of mud with a rank smell. The houses on Eleventh Street still had water lapping at their doorsteps, but the ones they'd emptied yesterday were safe. They'd have to have water pumped out of the cellars, but at least it hadn't reached the first floor. As soon as they could get the trucks in, volunteer firefighters would begin the pumping process. It'd be a long job.

"You did come back."

Simon turned at the voice to find the elderly couple he'd met the day before. They were looking tired but considerably more cheerful than they previously had.

"I said I'd come back," he reminded the man. "How are you? Did you have a place to sleep?"

"Goodness, yes. Our friends have been so nice, and they said they'd come to help so we can get back to normal." The wife seemed so happy that Simon didn't have the heart to point out that the basement was most likely full of mud and water that it would begin to stink if it hadn't already.

"I told you my house hadn't flooded in fifty years," her husband said, interrupting. "Now don't forget your promise when the truck brings our furniture."

His wife hushed him disapprovingly, but Simon just smiled. "I'll be here. But just now I'd best see what they want me to do first."

His spirits lifting irrationally that they, at least, had been spared the worst, he went over to where the police were organizing volunteers.

With a job in hand, Simon helped remove the sandbags that had done their job. This spring had for sure been different than he'd expected. Different, but not really disappointing. There was work to be done, and he could do it.

More volunteers arrived as the morning went on. Josiah showed up, along with Simon's daad and brothers. With all those willing hands, the work went quickly, and they were soon diverted to unloading the furniture for the Tenth Street houses.

It seemed inevitable that he'd be carrying back in the furniture he'd carried out yesterday, with the same elderly man hovering over them to make sure he did it right.

He must have seen a resemblance between Simon and his father, because he stopped Simon to ask and be introduced.

"We're mighty thankful," he said,

shaking Daad's hand vigorously. "We didn't get any water in the house, like I said, though."

"Better safe than sorry," his wife added. She lowered her voice as her husband moved out of range. "He doesn't like to admit he needs help," she whispered. "Thank you. Thank you," she repeated, tears glistening in faded blue eyes. "God bless you."

Daad clapped him on the back as they moved on to the next job. "That's better than any pay," he said. "You did a gut thing for them."

"Lots of folks are," he protested. "Including you."

"And Lyddy," Daad said, glancing past him.

Simon turned to find Lyddy and her elderly admirers handing out sandwiches and drinks to both volunteers and victims.

"Yah." He watched her talking with people, expressing caring in every word and gesture. Everyone seemed to know her, or else they could respond to her warmth even without knowing her. He could only marvel at the woman she'd become.

"Lyddy's a fine girl," his father said, too casually. "I don't know what Aunt Bess would do without her. Or a lot of other people. Ain't so?" His raised his eyebrows, and Simon thought he recognized the look in his eyes.

"Don't tell me Aunt Bess has got you matchmaking, too," he groaned. "Yah, Lyddy's a wonderful gut person, but I'm not looking for a wife." He hoped that would end it.

Daad nodded, but he hadn't lost the twinkle in his eyes.

"Maybe you should be," he said, tossing the words back over his shoulder as he headed for the sandwiches and coffee.

Lydia went back to the coffee shop, feeling oddly flat. She'd seen Simon, but he'd made no effort to come over and speak to her.

Well, why should he? Seeing him every day was already having an effect if she expected attention from him in a situation like this. Sarah came back from the phone, looking pleased. "That was Mamm. She says Aunt Bess is coming home. She wants you to pack up some things for her. I wrote them down." Sarah handed her a list. "They'll stop and get them on the way home."

"Wonderful." She scanned the list. "How soon are they coming? Maybe I should get them ready before I start anything else."

"Mammi said she was going to the hospital now. Someone is driving and will take them back home."

Lydia nodded. "I'll do it now, if you can manage here."

No need to ask—Sarah was delighted to be left in charge. Holding the list, Lydia hurried up the stairs.

Hearing someone behind her, she turned to find Becky scrambling after her.

"I'll help," she said.

Smiling, Lydia took her hand. "Those must be your favorite words," she teased gently.

Becky dimpled. "I like to help better than anything." She stopped to consider with that grave look of hers. "Except maybe coloring."

Her careful honesty made Lydia feel small. How many adults could be as honest about themselves? She didn't think she could.

It wasn't hard to find the things on the list, since Elizabeth's bedroom and bathroom were as well-organized as every other aspect of her life. Lydia handed each item to Becky, who put it carefully in the small suitcase Elizabeth used for her rare trips.

Lydia found herself wondering, as they worked, if this illness spelled the end of Elizabeth's life here over her shop. Goodness knew that most of her kin had been trying for years to convince her to make her home with them. It might be the best thing she could so. But what would happen to the shop then?

"Lyddy?" Becky's voice interrupted her thoughts.

"Yah?"

"I heard someone talking," she said carefully, as if not wanting to say who, "and she said that Daadi should get married again so I would have a mammi. But I already have a mammi, even if she's in heaven."

Lydia had to clench her teeth to keep from saying what she thought about supposed adults who'd be so careless as to say that in front of a child. Several Amish women who baked for the shop had been in that morning, and she could guess which of them it had been. For Becky's sake, she had to move carefully now.

Becky tugged at her sleeve. "What did they mean?"

She was committed to being Becky's friend, and she had to be as honest as the child was.

"People sometimes say silly things," she began. "I'm sure they know that no one could replace your mammi. I expect they thought that if Daadi got married, it would be to someone who would love you and take care of you like a mammi would. Not replace her but try hard to do what she would do."

She looked for signs of understanding in the small face. Becky nodded slowly.

"Do you think Daadi will?" she asked.

Another difficult question that required an honest answer. "I don't think so," she said. "At least, not right now. But you could talk to him about it."

Becky considered that. "Maybe not right now," she said, echoing Lydia's phrase.

That seemed to finish their conversation, so Lydia checked the list one last time and snapped the suitcase closed. "Okay, we're finished," she said. "Denke."

Together they walked out of the room, only to find Simon looking into one of the kitchen cabinets. Lydia's stomach clenched. Was she never to have a conversation with Becky that he didn't overhear? She braced herself for a lecture on the subject of minding her own business.

But none came. Simon seemed occupied by something else. "I just came in when Mammi called again. She's up at the hospital getting Aunt Bess ready to leave, and she says Bess wants some of her special tea. Do you know what that is? I don't see it."

Relieved, she reached into the cabinet he had opened. The tin was right in front of him.

"It's this one. An herbal blend that she

makes with mint and ginger. Was there anything else?"

"Not now," he said, relaxing. "But I imagine there will be something else about every day for a while."

Lydia almost asked him if he thought his aunt would be giving up the shop, but stopped herself, first because he might consider it interfering but also because she felt sure he wouldn't know, any more than she did. She headed down the stairs, very aware of him behind her and knowing she'd be waiting the rest of the day for him to tackle her about what he'd overheard.

Chapter Thirteen

Lydia stood outside the shop with Becky, waving as Elizabeth rode off looking like a queen, ensconced in the back seat with blankets and pillows around her. Becky waved energetically, but she was easily distracted when Lydia suggested they bake some cookies.

"I'm going to help make cookies," she announced when she entered the kitchen, heading straight for the oven.

"Yah, but we wash our hands first before touching food. Ain't so?"

Becky nodded, hurrying to the sink and standing on tiptoe to reach the faucet. Lydia watched her affectionately. What a wonderful thing it was to see Becky so happy and sure of herself. It was too bad that Elizabeth wasn't here to see it.

Her mind immediately switched gear to what would happen to the shop if Elizabeth didn't feel able to come back. She could always get another job, of course, but it wouldn't be the same. She'd always felt part of the business here with Elizabeth. No one else was likely to treat her so.

She shook the thought away irritably and set out to make a big batch of snickerdoodle cookies with Becky. As they stirred and rolled the cookies into balls, Becky kept up a steady stream of chatter. It was as if she were making up for all the silent days at one time. Once they got a couple of trays in the oven she waited, watching the oven doors anxiously.

"They're fine," Lydia assured her. "We have to give them time to bake."

"You're sure they'll be crinkly on top?"

"You know, I always used to wonder how they got that way," she said, smiling at Becky's surprise that Lydia should have worried about that, too. "I still don't know, but I know they always do."

That seemed to be good enough for Becky. She stepped back immediately when Lydia asked her to, holding her breath until the first tray of cookies was on the rack. She stood on tiptoe to check them out.

"They are crinkly," she crowed. "We did it."

"We certainly did." Grabbing a spatula, Lydia lifted the first cookie out, putting it on a small plate for Becky. "Mind you let it cool until I tell you it's okay. We don't want a burned tongue, now, do we."

Becky nodded solemnly, trying to look down at her tongue, and making Lydia laugh at the resulting expression. For a moment she wished Simon hadn't gone back to the work site so that he could enjoy the fun. But if he were, it would be hard to stop...

The bell on the front door jingled, and not sure where Sarah was, Lydia settled Becky at the table with her cookie and hurried through the swinging door.

Ella Burkhalter came through, carrying a large basket carefully. "Ach, Lyddy, I hope these rolls aren't down to crumbs by now. I wanted to bring something along to help, but the road is still torn up out our way."

"That's so kind of you, Ella. Everyone has helped so much—" She lost her voice at that point, because the person behind Ella was not her daughter but her niece, Judith Burkhalter.

"I'll put some of these in the kitchen,"

Ella said. "The rest can go in the display case if there's room."

"Yah, for sure." Lydia gathered together her straying wits. "Go ahead."

Ella hustled into the kitchen, leaving her alone with Judith. Intentionally? She didn't suppose she'd ever know.

Judith didn't speak for a few minutes. Then she walked closer. "I see you're taking care of everyone, like always."

Lydia felt as if she'd been hit in the face. "I don't know what you mean…" she began, but stopped when Judith began shaking her head, her lips trembling.

"I'm sorry." Judith sucked in a breath and seemed to steady herself. "I didn't mean to do that. That's not why I came."

Lydia put her hand on the counter, thankful the shop was empty at the moment. "Why did you come?" She didn't mean to sound curt, but she wasn't going to put herself through another nasty scene with Judith.

Judith pressed her fingers against her lips for a moment before she spoke. "Since I saw you at worship..." she stopped, then started again. "My aunt was ashamed of me. And I don't blame her. I never meant to be that way, but being back here and seeing you just made me relive that awful time. Seeing Thomas lying there—"

Her voice stumbled, and she stopped. Lydia found she couldn't hold on to her defenses for another moment. She moved quickly to put her arm around the girl, feeling the sobs she was trying to choke back.

"Komm. We'll sit down here. You don't have to tell me anything if you don't want to."

Judith sat where she indicated, and in a little while the sobs died away. "I do," she whispered. "Want to, I mean."

Nodding with as much encouragement as she could manage, Lydia sat down, glad to hear Becky's voice chattering about the snickerdoodle cookies.

"Thomas is doing much better," Judith finally said. "He got a very good doctor, and he's on some medicine that helps him a lot. I never thought… I mean, I believed he did that because of you. I thought you hurt him. None of us understood that he had something wrong with him. My mother and father felt so guilty once they understood."

Guilt and sorrow could be a powerful combination. Like Simon, still feeling responsible for Rebecca's death even though he wasn't to blame.

"I'm sorry," she said. "But he's better now?"

Judith nodded, dabbing her eyes with a tissue. "He works with Daad on the farm, and he got Daad to plant an orchard that's doing wonderful good. He's even talking about maybe getting married to a woman who lives just down the road."

"I'm glad," she said, wondering how much her brother's marriage plans had upset his devoted sister. "If I'd been wiser, I might have been able to handle the situation better."

Judith sniffed into her tissue. "Yah. I guess we all have something to be sorry about."

She decided against responding to those words. She didn't want to say anything that might make Judith flare up again.

"I just hope he's not making a mistake again." Judith seemed to be talking to herself.

Lydia leaned back in her chair, hoping this had done Judith some good. It hadn't felt very pleasant to her, but it seemed the least she could do.

"I suppose you think I'm being silly." Judith darted a look at her, sounding sulky.

"No, not a bit. He's your bruder, and you love him."

Apparently, that was the right thing to say, because Judith gave a sudden nod and stood up. "I'll find my aunt," she muttered and turned away.

She seemed so incredibly young to Lydia, even younger than she was. It was as if her brother's troubles had become hers, and Judith had gotten stuck back in the past.

Poor girl. If Lydia had harbored any resentment against her for the scene at worship, it was completely gone now. All she could feel was pity.

With Aunt Bess in his mother's capable hands and Sarah and Lyddy in charge at the shop, Simon found himself at loose ends. He'd go back to the work he'd started in the shop, but it seemed wrong to enjoy himself with the old clock he'd rescued when other people were in such trouble. So, with a quick goodbye, he went back down to the flood zone to see if he could find something useful to do.

He reached the corner where he could see down to the creek, and as he did, his father joined him.

"Aunt Bess is settled at home already," he said, before Simon could ask the question. "It went okay, so I got dropped back here."

Simon grinned. "You mean you want to get out of the way of Mammi fussing over Aunt Bess."

"That's about it," he admitted. "Not that Aunt Bess doesn't deserve some fussing over. She's always doing for other folks, but she doesn't want anyone doing for her."

He nodded, knowing how true that was, and they both turned to survey the scene in front of them. The creek was still muddy, but it had gone down visibly since earlier in the day, allowing people to see the row of houses that had been flooded. Stained and muddy, some with porches swept away, they were still standing.

Nearby, an older couple stood, obviously looking down at the houses that had just emerged from the water. Even as Simon watched, the woman's tears began to flow.

"How will we ever get it back to the way it was?" She began to weep, seeming too distraught to care who heard her, and Simon's throat tightened with sympathy.

He turned away, not wanting to stare. "Those poor people," he murmured.

"Yah." Daad nodded to where the other volunteers were gathering. "Best thing we can do for them is put in a couple of hours' work, ain't so?"

Daad was right, of course, but it was frustrating to see neighbors in such distress and not be able to do more.

They joined a group that was sweeping water and mud from one of the houses where the basement had been flooded.

It was muddy, smelly work, but at least it was something.

After a half hour, the fireman in charge of the crew called a halt. "Everybody outside and breathe some fresh air for a few minutes. We need it."

They all trooped outside, and most of them sat down on a convenient log fence. Muddy and wet, it was still better than standing.

There was a little flurry of movement down by the lower houses, with a small group advancing on one of them. Simon looked a question at the firefighter.

"They're starting to let folks in for a look at the damage," he said. "Not that they can do anything about it now." He shrugged. "Still, they want to see the worst."

Judging by the way people looked as they came away, there'd been nothing good to see.

"Wish I could do more," the firefighter muttered. "Guess we all wish that. Still, there's been no loss of life. We have to be thankful of that."

Daad nodded. "There's always something to be thankful for. But they're grieving the life they knew and most likely the memories they lost."

"I guess I was just thinking about the physical loss," Simon admitted. "But I know what you mean about the life they lost. That's what it's been for me and Becky. Not just Rebecca, but the whole life we built together."

He regretted saying it at once. Daad had never been one to talk about his feelings. He'd probably be embarrassed...

But his father put a comforting hand on his shoulder. "You and Becky still have each other. You'll build a home, maybe marry again. Not forget but move on."

"I don't think so." Simon stared absently at the scene in front of them. "I can't love anyone else the way I loved Rebecca."

His father's hand tightened on his shoulder, and Simon sensed that he was struggling to speak. He actually hoped he wouldn't. There was nothing anyone could say that would change how he felt.

But Daad wasn't done with him. "Not the same way, maybe." His voice was husky. "But you can still love someone. Marriage isn't just for the young, remember. Folks get married for companionship, or for family, or just to have someone to take care of. God still blesses them."

Simon sat silently until they were called to return to work. He'd never heard Daad speak that way before and probably never would again. He'd retire back into his taciturn manner and stay there.

Maybe that was why it had made such a strong impression. He didn't agree— didn't think it was possible. But if it could…that was something to ponder, wasn't it?

* * *

To Lydia's relief, the next few days saw a return to something like normal, although the people who'd lost the most likely didn't see it that way. She and Sarah were still providing coffee and treats to the volunteers and the emergency shelter, and Simon, like a lot of others, worked several hours a day in the flood zone.

It was a measure of how much the conditions had improved that Jim Jacobs, the water treatment plant manager, was actually there ordering his usual coffee and cruller.

"Nice to be able to come out in public without worrying someone will punch me." He grinned as he handed her the cash.

"It wasn't so bad as that, surely. Still, when you're used to turning the spigot and having water come out..."

"I know, I know. We worked twenty-four hours a day, but the pumps had to be rebuilt." He grimaced. "Not easy, and how the town's budget is going to hold up, I don't know."

"You should have heard how folks cheered when the water came back on," she told him. "That would encourage you."

When he wasn't smiling, Jim looked drawn and tired. "I kept thinking there should be more I could do."

"Probably we all felt that." She thought about Simon's frustration at not being able to do more. And her own, feeling much the same. "We can each only do our part and trust God for the rest, ain't so?"

Jim nodded, picking up the bag with his coffee and cruller. "I'll try to remember that."

Lydia stood musing for a moment on how strange it was. She'd heard the same thing from so many of the volunteers, working twelve hours a day but wanting to do more and feeling helpless against the flood. But on the other side were the complainers, who did nothing. An emergency seemed to bring out the best in some folks and the worst in others.

She automatically checked on Becky and found her drying teaspoons and arranging them neatly in the drawer. Her heart warmed. Becky had the ability, rare in a five-year-old, of concentrating fully on a task until it was finished. It had taken her younger siblings another ten years to manage that, as she remembered.

Finishing, Becky closed the drawer and hung her towel up neatly. As she looked up, she caught Lydia's eyes on her and smiled. Skipping over to her, she caught Lydia's hand.

"Could you help me with my sewing? Please?"

Lydia had started her off on a sewing project a few days earlier, and Becky was an apt pupil. Her neat fingers took to handling a needle quickly.

"Yah, let's do that." A glance told her that Sarah had everything under control. She reached for the sewing basket she'd put on a shelf, and Becky led the way to her usual small table near the kitchen door.

"Do you think you can finish your heart pillow today?" They'd been working on a small pink heart shape which would become a pillow when stuffed with foam.

Checking the stitches to be sure they were lined up, she put it on the table and smoothed it out. "Just keep on stitching until you get right here." She put a straight pin in to mark the spot. "Remember how to make a knot at the end?"

"I remember," Becky said, her face scrunching up. "I think. But maybe you'd better do it."

"I will." Lydia touched her cheek lightly, thinking how much she'd miss the child when she wasn't seeing Becky every day—to say nothing of not seeing Simon.

He'd gone out to see Aunt Bess after lunch, and he hadn't returned yet. There should be nothing to make her tense in his visit, but she couldn't seem to help herself. She kept waiting to hear that his great-aunt was giving up the shop. And in the process giving up Lyddy's job.

It didn't necessarily mean that, she knew. Even if she sold or turned the shop over to someone else in the family, Lydia might be able to keep working. Might, but might not. Whoever took over the shop could have family of their own to help run it.

For a moment she toyed with the idea that she might be able to buy it herself, but what would she use for money? She'd saved some, but not enough. Daad would help her if she asked, but she wasn't going to ask. He had the others to establish, and she could take care of herself.

"Ready," Becky said, taking her mind off herself. She held out the fleece heart, its bright pink a cheerful contrast to her dark green dress.

"Okay." She took the fabric, making a small knot at the end of Becky's sewing. "Now you get to stuff it."

Becky clapped her hands. "I want to do it."

Pulling out the plastic bag filled with foam, Lydia showed her how to poke each piece through the hole she'd left, pushing it into the farthest part of the pillow first. Giggling a little, Becky pulled out a handful of foam and began pressing it in.

"And then we sew the hole closed and it's done, ain't so?" Becky said eagerly. "I want to give it to Aunt Bess. Do you think she'll like it?"

Lydia blinked back a tear at the child's thoughtfulness. "I know she'll love it. That's a wonderful gut idea."

She was kneeling next to Becky's

chair, helping her, when she glanced up to see Simon standing a few feet away, watching them with the strangest expression on his face.

Standing up quickly, Lydia took a step toward him. "What is it? Is something wrong with your aunt?"

"No, no, there's nothing wrong." Whatever had been troubling him, Simon seemed to wipe it away quickly. "Aunt Bess is a little stronger every day. Today she even asked if we've started filling up the freezer again." He hesitated. "I told her yes, but are we?"

Lydia laughed at his expression. "Yah, we have." She tried to take her mind off her own worries. "Look what Becky is making."

Becky held it up with a smile of satisfaction. "See? It's almost finished. I'm going to give it to Aunt Bess. Lyddy says she'll like it."

"Lyddy's right," he said, smiling at his daughter with a tenderness that melted

Lydia's heart. "She'll love it. You're doing a wonderful gut job."

He sat down next to Becky, and Lydia murmured an excuse and headed for the kitchen. She treasured seeing him each day, but sitting there with him and his daughter suddenly overwhelmed her with emotion. That was too intimate for her control.

The rest of the afternoon she managed to keep too busy to have any time to spare thinking about either Simon or the possibility of losing her job. Gradually her emotions returned to normal, and she was able to take her usual interest in her customers. Everyone had a story to tell about how they'd weathered the flood, and in some ways they almost took pride in the fact of having survived.

Also, the bond that had formed when the people of Lost Creek struggled with the flood seemed to make them a more tightly knit community. She was reminded of the Israelites fleeing Egypt, growing stronger as a people from the hardships they faced.

Closing time came soon enough, and she was pleased to see Sarah moving through the routine with the efficiency of an expert. She remembered the conversation they'd had earlier and decided that Sarah was certainly proving that she was growing up.

When Lydia said her goodbyes and headed for the stable, she was surprised to find Simon walking along beside her. When she glanced at him questioningly, he shrugged, his face serious.

"I'll help you harness up." That was all he said, but she felt as if something troubling lurked beneath the surface.

She unhooked the stall door and paused for a moment before leading Dolly out. "If there's something wrong, I wish you'd tell me." She managed to say it without looking at him.

"There's nothing wrong." He bit off

the words and then took a deep breath. "I have something to ask you."

Lydia looked up, startled. "What is it?"

Simon sucked in another breath. "Lydia, will you marry me?"

Chapter Fourteen

Lydia could only stand there, shocked and stunned beyond belief. Simon had spoken the words she thought she'd never hear. Asked her the question she'd imagined but hadn't expected. Why was she standing there speechless when he was offering her the gift she'd always dreamed of?

Because there was something wrong. Shouldn't Simon be looking at her with love in his eyes when he said those words? Instead, he stood holding Dolly's halter with one hand and patting her with the other. She could almost convince herself she'd imagined it.

He cleared his throat, sent a flickering glance her way, and then concentrated on the mare again. "I guess I shouldn't have sprung it on you that way. But I've been thinking it over. I mean, we're so well suited to each other. We've known each other since we were children… know everything there is to know, I guess." He stopped to take a breath after getting that much out. "You'll think this is sudden, but I know some of what folks say is true—I do need a wife. There's Becky, and I shouldn't keep her from having a normal life because of what I feel."

Lydia's sense that this was all wrong increased. She managed to make her lips form the words. "What do you feel?"

Again that quick, sidelong glance that flickered away almost before it landed. "Guess you know as well as anyone what my feelings were about Rebecca.

I can't love anyone else the way I loved her. But Daad pointed out to me that folks get married for a lot of reasons other than falling in love. There's friendship, and family, and...well, just having somebody."

Anybody. Her numbed mind formed the word. Anybody would do...well, any mature Amish woman with a gift for making a home and the heart to love another woman's child.

He'd seen her so often with Becky. He must have realized how close they were getting, and from that it was a simple step to finding a way to make it permanent. That is, as long as he could keep love out of the equation.

Her heart had been growing heavier and heavier, and now it felt as if it would sink to her toes. Simon had said they knew each other. Maybe that was true for her, but he didn't know her all that well, not when he didn't understand what he meant to her.

And he must never know. If he even guessed, it would be the ultimate humiliation. She felt as if he'd put a beautiful, fragile gift in her outstretched hands and then dashed it to the floor, breaking it into a thousand pieces.

Somehow, she had to prevent him from knowing the truth. Summoning all her strength, she forced her voice to stay calm.

"No." After she got that out, the rest was easier, and like him, she found it better to stare at Dolly. "Denke, Simon, but I can't."

He didn't visibly react, although she thought he grew a little more rigid. His hand fell from the halter, and he took a step back, giving a short nod.

"Denke. I'm sorry if I embarrassed you."

She ought to say something in reply, but she knew she couldn't. She couldn't even watch as he walked away.

Forcing herself to hold back the sobs

that threatened to rip her apart, she harnessed the mare with shaking fingers. She had to get somewhere to break down in decent privacy. Not the house, that was certain sure. But the daadi haus—Grossmammi wouldn't badger her with questions and comments and sympathy that didn't help. Grossmammi would allow her to be alone to let out all her grief and pain. That was all anyone could do for her right now.

Well, that was that. Simon muttered an excuse to Sarah and shut himself in his workroom. The old clock was still waiting on his table, and involving himself in its workings would be guaranteed to keep his mind occupied.

But for once, that didn't help. What was wrong with him? He'd tried, and he'd lost. He wasn't even especially surprised. After all, what did he have to offer a woman like Lyddy? She was still hardly more than a girl, probably still hoping for a prince to carry her off to her happily-ever-after.

All he had to offer was a life of cooking and cleaning and looking after children. She'd probably rather continue the job she already had and hold on to her life of freedom. And what right did he have to deprive her of the chance at that wonderful head-over-heels, walking-on-air feeling of first love. He'd already had it, but she hadn't.

Annoyed with himself, he picked up the tiny screwdriver he used to loosen the parts inside the clock. But his fingers seemed to have lost their cunning, and all he succeeded in doing was breaking off the first screw. He slammed the screwdriver down on the table, and the end of it snapped off.

He shoved his chair back and surged to his feet. He'd best find something else to do before he ruined the clock and his tools. Striding to the door, Simon hesitated before turning the knob.

Lyddy would be gone by now. He could go and help Sarah with the cleanup and not worry about seeing Lyddy. Maybe by tomorrow she'd have forgotten the whole stupid thing, and they'd be able to go on as they had been. But he doubted it.

Still, the next day it seemed he was right. Lyddy appeared to be as calm and pleasant as if the previous day hadn't happened. He should be glad. He was glad, he assured himself.

The only problem was that Lyddy seemed to be...well, evading him, he guessed. When he came into the kitchen, she found a reason to hurry out front. If he walked behind the counter, she picked up her pad and dashed off to check on her tables.

The third time it happened, Simon realized it wasn't his imagination. That must mean that despite her cheerful expression, his untimely proposal had made things awkward between them.

He'd apologize again, but he didn't have a chance. Lyddy was very skilled at making sure they were never alone together.

By late morning it had become so evident that he decided he'd be better off going down to the flood zone, even though he wasn't scheduled to work until two in the afternoon. He caught Sarah on her way through the kitchen.

"I'm going to head down to work now unless you need me for anything. You'll look after Becky, ain't so?"

"For sure, but what about the shed? You said you'd clean it out for us today."

"I'll do it tomorrow," he said shortly, eager to go now that he'd made his decision. If Lyddy didn't want to be alone with him, he'd remove himself.

Sarah frowned. "Don't you remember? We have a big shipment of paper products due this afternoon, now that the trucks can get through. You'll have to make space for them."

"Stop nagging," he snapped. "I'll get to it before tomorrow."

"What's wrong? Why are you so short-tempered today?"

"I'm not." He practically snarled the words, halfway out the door.

"Then I'd hate to see you when you are."

Simon frowned at her. His little sister had grown disagreeably outspoken, it seemed to him.

"Later," he said, keeping his voice calm with an effort. He was out the door before she could say another thing.

The trouble was, sassy or not, Sarah was right. So he trudged into the shed and made quick work of clearing up so the delivery guy could get at the shelves. The jugs that had been used for carrying water in would have to be returned to their owners, but that, at least, could wait.

He was welcomed with open arms at the flood zone, since one of the other volunteers had had to switch his time to afternoon. Relieved, Simon set to work. Shoveling mud out of someone's basement seemed a lot better than trying to stay out of Lyddy's way, and by the time he'd put in a few hours of hard labor, he'd worked off most of his ill humor.

Sarah had been right, of course. He'd been taking his feelings out on anyone who was handy, and that wasn't fair. And now he owed her an apology, as well. He'd certain sure done a fine job of making things worse.

It didn't make any sense to be so put out about Lyddy's answer. So she had turned him down. He'd known that was a possibility. It wasn't as if his heart was involved, so why was he so distressed?

By the time Simon returned to the shop, he was determined to be pleasant to everyone if it killed him. His resolution was tested immediately by his sister's approach.

"There you are at last," Sarah said,

looking at him as if he'd missed something crucial. "Aunt Bess called twice while you were gone, asking for you."

"Is something wrong?" But if her illness were worse, someone else would surely have called.

Sarah shrugged. "She didn't say. She just said to tell you to get out there this afternoon. She has to see you."

He opened his mouth to object, but a glance at Sarah told him she wasn't going to be sympathetic. "All right." He glanced down at his clothes, splattered with mud and worse. "I'll clean up and go. All right?"

Sarah shrugged again. "Fine with me," she said, and hustled off with a tray of cups.

Stopping only to greet his daughter and admire the picture she was making, he tramped upstairs to shower and change, just managing to catch a glimpse of Lyddy at a table in the very front of the shop.

By the time he came back down, it was closing time, and Sarah was locking the front door. "Lyddy just left," she said, even though he hadn't asked.

Mindful of how testy he'd been earlier, he managed to smile. "Can I help you clean up?"

Becky answered. "I'm helping," she pointed out.

Sarah smiled. "That's right. Becky and I can do it. You get along before Aunt Bess calls again."

With a quick wave, he headed out to the stable, revolving in his mind the possible things that might have upset his aunt. He reached the double doors and realized that Lyddy hadn't left yet. She was still harnessing Dolly.

He stopped, unsure what to say. "Sorry. I mean, I'm heading out your way, too. Aunt Bess wants to see me." Lifting the harness from its peg, he approached the gelding.

"Yah, I heard," she said, not looking

at him. "I'll be out of your way in two shakes."

"No need to hurry. In fact, if you'll wait a minute, I'll follow you home, just in case." In case of what, he didn't know.

"You can't," she said quickly. "I mean, I'm not going your way. I'm heading out to see my cousin Beth."

Simon took a deep breath, trying to find the words that would make things normal again. "Lyddy—"

But she'd already swung up to the buggy seat. "I'll see you tomorrow." She snapped the lines and rushed off as if she were being chased. Obviously she didn't want to talk to him—now or later.

Lydia hadn't intended to go to Beth's until she said the words, and then she realized that seeing Beth was exactly what she needed right now. She and Beth had gone through so much together, from childhood mischief to teenage crushes to the death of Beth's husband and the discovery of his betrayal. She had been with Beth through that trying time, and she knew instinctively that Beth would want to walk through this desolate valley with her.

When she tugged the line to turn away from home, Dolly shook her head, making the harness jingle. In Dolly's opinion, it was time they went home.

"Not today," she said firmly. "We have another call to make first." Confiding in the mare might be foolish, but there were times when she needed to speak without being careful of what she said—the way she had to be with Simon.

Lydia's throat grew tight at the thought of his name, but she shook it off much as Dolly had tried to shake off her directions. She didn't want to have herself so upset that she burst into tears at the sight of her cousin. So she forced herself to concentrate on mundane things like how many doughnuts they'd need the next day.

It wasn't far to Beth's place. Lydia turned in the lane next to the country store that Beth and Daniel owned, hoping Beth was at the house rather than busy in the store.

A moment's thought reassured her. At this hour, Beth was likely to be in the kitchen getting supper started. Sure enough, when she pulled up at the house, Beth came hurrying out with a welcoming smile. But the smile faded as soon as she got a look at Lydia's face. She put her arm around Lydia's waist and led her into the house.

"It's all right. We're all alone, and you can tell me. Was ist letz? What's wrong? Is it Simon?"

The tears started to flow as soon as she saw Beth's caring face, and she wiped them away impatiently. She'd cried enough.

"Yah, it was Simon." She sank into a chair, feeling the need of something to hold her up. "He asked me to marry him."

Beth took the chair next to her and took Lydia's hand in hers. "That's usually a happy thing. Are you going to tell me you don't love him?"

She shook her head. "That's the problem. I do love him. But Simon was very honest. He's not looking for love. He's looking for a good Amish woman who'll be his helpmate and a mother to Becky." She stopped, pressing her fingers to her temples. Holding back tears guaranteed a headache, it seemed.

"He never said that to you." The indignation in her cousin's voice warmed Lydia's heart. "He wouldn't."

"Oh, yes, he would. He did."

"You should have hit him with something."

Clearly, gentle, sweet Beth was angry enough for both of them. Too bad Lydia didn't feel anger. It would probably be easier than the desolation in her heart.

"I couldn't," she murmured. "It hurt too much."

"My dear." Beth put her arms around Lydia, patting her back as she might a small child who'd skinned his knee and required comforting. "I'm so sorry. The first time you fall in love, and it has to be with someone who's so wrapped up in the past that he can't see what's right in front of him. You'd be perfect for him."

Beth's anger for her pain and her comforting touch were doing their work. Lydia began to feel that she'd live through this.

"That's exactly what he thinks. That I'd be the perfect stepmother and the perfect housekeeper. Nothing more."

"Ach, that's so foolish. Does he think you'll sit around waiting until he comes to his senses?"

Lyddy leaned back in the chair, feeling spent. "I don't think he ever will. He's still in love with Rebecca." Another tear escaped, and she dashed it away. "Anyway, I can't stay where I'm going to see him every day. I'll have to get another job." She hadn't really thought that out, but she knew it was true. She didn't want to go through any more days like this one.

Beth squeezed her hands tightly. "But I thought this was just temporary. Simon having his workshop at the store, I mean. I'd hate to see you give up a job you love."

What Beth said was true. This was never intended to be long-term on Simon's part. But then again, his aunt might decide to give up the store, and she'd have to find another job anyway.

"I don't know," she said, uncertain of the way forward. "I guess I can't walk away while Elizabeth is sick, can I?"

"That's certain sure." Beth's hands gentled, patting hers. "Why don't you try to hang in there a little longer, anyway? Just until you see what everyone's plans are. After all, you can make a point of avoiding him, can't you?"

"I guess so." With Simon off several hours each day volunteering, it shouldn't be that difficult. And she could be training Sarah to take her place in the event she did decide to move on.

"I wouldn't think it that difficult. After all, he must be feeling embarrassed and awkward around you anyway. Ain't so?"

She nodded. Beth was right, and just talking it over with her had made Lydia feel better. Stronger, and more able to cope with whatever came. She couldn't possibly walk out on Elizabeth when she was ill.

"You're right," she said, coming to a decision. "I'll have to do it. I don't have any other choice."

"Maybe…well, maybe Simon will realize what he's missing. It could happen, couldn't it?"

She hated to dash Beth's dreams of happily-ever-after for her, but she knew they were futile. "Perhaps," she said. "But as far as I can see, Simon is still in love with Rebecca. And I don't think that will ever change."

It was a hard thing to accept, but she had to do it and move on. If she didn't she'd be like Simon, stuck in the past in an endless loop of grief and guilt. And that wasn't how she wanted to live. No, she would heal from this. But it was going to take a long, long time.

Chapter Fifteen

Since Becky was very occupied in helping Sarah to close the coffee shop, Simon didn't suggest she go with him to see Aunt Bess. Instead, he drove out the road alone, stopping for a moment at the point where the old lane led off to the right. The barricade ahead of him sealed the spot where the road had collapsed. Looking at the creek now as it tumbled gently over rocks in the stream bed, he had a vivid image in his mind of Lyddy's buggy rocking perilously in the raging current, while Lyddy struggled to get the mare to safety.

His heart gave an uncomfortable thud at the picture. Would she have gotten out if he hadn't come along just then? Maybe, but thank the gut Lord he had. It was a wonderful example of how the Lord cared for each one.

With a silent prayer of thanksgiving, he turned onto the lane and made his way over the rutted surface toward the farm. It got a little worse each day, and another load of gravel might not be enough. The highway department probably hadn't even considered this small area in the midst of the damage the flood had done.

Arriving at the house, he greeted everyone and then hurried to the bedroom where Aunt Bess was waiting. Waiting impatiently, he realized as soon as he saw her face.

"It took you long enough," she snapped.

He didn't find it hard to see that her forced confinement was hard on Aunt Bess's nerves. She was always one to be up and doing, not taking it easy as the doctor had said she must.

"The way through the woods is in pretty bad shape. There's no way to take it at a trot, that's certain sure."

She nodded, but she didn't look mollified. Frowning, she pointed to a straight chair that was across from the rocker she occupied. "Sit down there and account for yourself. What did you say to get Lyddy so upset?"

At first he could only gape at her. He'd never thought Lyddy would talk about it. "How did you find out?"

"Lyddy's grossmammi got it out of her after she came home weeping her eyes out."

Lyddy, weeping because of what he had said to her? The words felt like a punch in the heart.

"I... I don't understand. She seemed to be all right when she left the shop. I'd never have guessed she'd be upset." He remembered the calm with which she'd turned him down.

"You were wrong. What exactly did you say?"

He suspected he wasn't going to be forgiven very quickly for this misstep. And he guessed he didn't deserve to be forgiven, but how could he have known it would perturb her that much?

"I asked her to marry me. I said we'd known each other from childhood, and we got along well, and I knew how much she cared about Becky. And I told her what Daad said—"

He stopped, because Aunt Bess's expression said he shouldn't quote Daad.

"Go on," she snapped. "What did your daad say?"

"He...he said that...well, that there were lots of reasons for getting married besides falling in love." Under her critical gaze, he stumbled to a stop.

"First of all, don't ever follow another man's advice about women. Your father meant well, I guess." She made it sound like a bad thing. "Never mind what he said. What do you feel about Lydia?"

Thoughts tumbled around in his head. "I admire her. She's a wonderful good person—loving and sympathetic and always helping others. But as for love, I don't feel for Lyddy what I felt for Rebecca, and—"

"You're ferhoodled, that's what you are!" She smacked her hand on the arm of the rocker, looking like she'd like to smack something else. "For sure you don't feel what you felt for Rebecca. You're not seventeen now. You're not a boy, waiting to tumble head over heels in love."

She started to cough, alarming him. "Aunt Bess, don't upset yourself. I'd better leave. We can talk later."

"Yah, you go away." She glared at him, and he winced. "Go away and think about how you feel when you're with

Lyddy. And then ask yourself how you'd feel if you never saw Lyddy again."

The words snatched his breath away for a moment. Before he could speak, she went on.

"If you ever figure out what you want, then tell her what that is, starting with your feelings."

"I couldn't, even if I wanted to," he said, unwilling to say another word about his feelings and searching for an excuse. "She hasn't let me get anywhere near her, and I don't think she will."

Aunt Bess looked at him, shaking her head as if he'd given a foolish answer. "That's something you'll have to figure out for yourself. There's always a way if you want something badly enough. Now go away and do some thinking."

Chastened, Simon headed back toward town, carefully avoiding the worst of the ruts and holes. He appreciated Aunt Bess's caring. He did. And he was sorry he'd made Lyddy cry. But he couldn't…

He'd made Lyddy cry. The words surrounded his heart, squeezing it without mercy. He'd made her cry.

What was it Aunt Bess had said? *Think about how you feel when you're with Lyddy.* That was easy enough to answer, wasn't it? He felt warm, safe, understood, happy. And he wanted to be with her more and more.

But that wasn't love—at least, it wasn't what he had felt when he'd fallen in love with Rebecca. Aunt Bess had made short work of that reasoning, hadn't she?

He'd reached the blacktop road. Once again he stopped, staring at the creek, remembering. And hearing Aunt Bess's words again. *Ask yourself how you'd feel if you never saw Lyddy again.*

Eyes fixed on the swirling water, he found his thoughts swirling as if they were being tumbled in the creek the way Lyddy's buggy had been. He seemed to see Lyddy back in the raging waters, being swept away and out of his sight while he stood helpless, unable to save her.

And then the truth overwhelmed him until he felt as if he were drowning in it.

He knew now what he wanted. He wanted Lyddy, not because she'd be a good mother to Becky but because she was as important to him as breathing. But after the mistake he'd made, how could he ever convince Lyddy?

By the next morning, Lydia still wasn't sure how many of her family members knew what had happened. She hadn't thought to urge Grossmammi to keep it quiet, but she'd know it wasn't the sort of thing Lyddy would want drifting around the community.

Judging by the sympathetic glances Mammi was sending her way as she ate breakfast, Mammi must know. But at least she wasn't talking about it. That was the last thing Lyddy wanted right now. She was still too close to the edge of tears for anything like that.

Josiah started to ask her something, but Daad caught his attention and sent his mind off in another direction. Thank the good Lord. One day this would fade from her memory, and she'd be able to talk about Simon, and to Simon, in a normal way. But that day seemed very, very far away.

As soon as possible, Lyddy set out for town. She wasn't looking forward to seeing Simon, but she was responsible for keeping the coffee shop running, and she lived up to her responsibilities. Given how embarrassed he'd seemed the previous day, she could hope that Simon would find things to do that kept him out of her vicinity.

Beth had been right to urge patience. Simon wasn't going to be at the shop forever, and once he'd moved, she'd see very little of him. She shouldn't have to give up a job she enjoyed just because he had spoken out of turn.

Fortified by her thoughts, she followed the lane down toward the spot where it joined the road. The surface was worse here, probably because excess rainfall was flowing down the hill toward the stream. Daad had been talking about getting together with the neighbors to put another load of gravel on it, tamping it down firmly. He seemed to think very little of the chances the state would get at the job soon. Simon's daad would be wanting to help, no doubt.

Her thoughts occupied, Lydia rounded a stand of dense pines and found the blacktop road in sight. Just where the lane joined the road, a buggy stood, half-on, half-off the lane. A buggy she recognized—Simon's buggy. And Simon was on the ground next to the front wheel.

Lydia didn't think. She just ran, jumping from the buggy even before the mare came to a halt, and raced toward him. If Simon was hurt…

As she neared him, he rose, and in another moment she felt his arms close around her, holding her as if he'd never let go. She felt his heart beating with hers—his breath moving in rhythm with hers. She couldn't think; she could only feel.

"Are you all right? You weren't hurt?" She managed to gasp out the words.

A rumble sounded in his chest as he chuckled. "Not hurt just sliding off the seat, that's certain sure. I cut the corner too sharp and slid right into the ditch." He pressed his cheek against hers. "Serves me right for teasing you about your driving." His arms tightened convulsively. "Lyddy," he murmured, his voice roughening. "Forgive me."

She leaned back just enough to look into his face, and what she saw there silenced all her doubts.

"I will always forgive you." She knew

she was making a promise to last a life-time. "I love you." It was such a relief to say the words, to express the feeling that surged through her at his touch and his nearness.

"I love you." He moved, cupping her face in his hands and looking into her eyes. "I love you, and I was so foolish. I didn't even recognize love when I saw it."

She could smile now, any smidgen of doubt chased away for good. "What made you see?"

"Aunt Bess." He made a rueful grimace. "She always knows everything. She asked me how I would feel if I never saw you again." His palms pressed against her cheeks. "I couldn't bear it. I knew in an instant. If you went away, I couldn't..." His eyes filled with tears. She reached up to pull his face to hers.

"I won't," she said. "You have me for keeps."

His lips touched hers, and joy filled her heart. Simon had given her the most precious gift he could. He'd given her his love. On that gift they would build a family with Becky and whatever other children the Lord should send them. And every day she would thank God, the giver of all good gifts, for bringing them together.

* * * * *

If you enjoyed this story,
don't miss the previous books in the
Brides of Lost Creek series
from Marta Perry:

Second Chance Amish Bride
The Wedding Quilt Bride
The Promised Amish Bride
The Amish Widow's Heart

Find more great reads
at www.LoveInspired.com

Dear Reader,

I'm happy you picked up my new Lost Creek book. Whether you're new to Lost Creek or an old friend, welcome!

Lost Creek has become very real to me over the course of five books, and sometimes I forget that it comes from my imagination. This new story brings in some familiar characters and places while introducing new people, all drawn together in an emergency.

I've done flood stories before, but I find that when you've gone through it yourself, there's always something new to say. It's my experience that emergencies, whether they're weather events or epidemics, can bring out the very best in people as they rally to help one another through difficult times.

I hope you'll let me know how you liked my book, and do let me know if you'd like to receive a bookmark and my brochure of Pennsylvania Dutch recipes.

You can reach me at www.martaperry.com and on Facebook at www.facebook.com/martaperrybooks.

Blessings,

Marta Perry